HUSTLE2HARD
PUBLICATIONS PRESENTS

Fuck Love
I DIDN'T SIGN UP FOR THIS

By

Shoney K

This book is dedicated:

To all the women that have been hurt by love,
to all the women who believed all his lies,
and to all the women that ever screamed out
FUCK LOVE.
Ladies do know that things will get better.
Put GOD first and watch how he brings that man
in your life that knows your worth.

Special Shout Out to my Sis Venus, keep your head up!

<u>To my Supporters</u>
There have been numerous occasions that I have screamed
out fuck love. I'm not afraid to admit that I have been hurt,
used and abused, but my past has made me a stronger
person. I live my life without any regrets. Each day I get
stronger than the day I was before. Now that I have learned
to put my past behind me, I have finally found someone
that knows my worth, my heart and my soul as much as I
do. Yes, I'm happily in love and there's no better feeling in
life to know that you are appreciated and to know that
when you love someone, that someone loves you back.
Without my past experiences, there is no way I would be
able to appreciate and love the man that God has bought
into my life.

Now you are tuning in to a story that many women know
too well…

CHAPTER ONE

When a woman is fed up there is nothing you can do about it, I spoke softly to myself as I contemplated suicide, but it only took a minute to shake that shit off. Suicide, what was I thinking. I quickly gathered my thoughts, shook my head up and down, and said aloud, "That nigga deserved what he got." The more I heard myself say those words, the better it made me feel because there was no excuse for what he did to me. I tried to feel sorry for his sorry ass, but my mind wouldn't allow my heart to. See, a man is never supposed to play with a bitch heart like mines especially when I've given up everything for him. It's sad to say that he played pussy and got fucked double time, and now he's six feet under. I'm not going to lie though, I never imagined that the man I loved and the man I've given my all too blood would be on my hands. If only he would have loved me and only me, we wouldn't be in this situation.

As I lay on this hard ass bed, courtesy of Dwight Correction Facility, I thought about the good days that he and I shared. My heart began to soften as I imagined how he used to hold me in his arms at night and how he made me feel. Going down memory lane had tears forming in the wells of my eyes and then they trickled down my oval face. My happy thoughts were quickly replaced by the thoughts of the day I committed this horrific crime when I heard the correctional officer's voice disciplining my next-door cellmate. My heart began to sadden with every second that ticked away. My emotions were all over the place. I didn't know if I wanted to live or die. Those suicide thoughts that had escaped moments ago were back invading my head. The more I thought about what I've done, the more I sunk into a depressed state of mind. I tried to convince myself over and over again that he deserved what he got, but I couldn't. All I know is the damage was done and there was no turning back. Every time I closed my eyes there he was lying in a huge puddle of blood next to our bed. One shot to the head and two to the chest was all it took. I'm not going to lie, I can't. I do miss him. I miss everything about him, from his smile, his touch, to the smell of his cologne, down to his dirty drawers. I never pictured my life without him. He was my provider, my protector, my everything, he was my God, but I had to learn very quickly that God don't want no man before him and I believe this is why the devil exposed himself in my relationship. Now, I have the next sixty-five years of my life behind bars to think about the past, present and no future.

My life literally ended, the day I took Hodari's life and now I'm trying my best to get accustom to horrible food, a small smelly cell, twin size bunk bed, a sink and a toilet that I share with my cellmate Adrianna. All my cold and sleepless nights were shared with her and she was locked away for the same reason I was locked up for, killing in the name of love.

Money was what the streets called him, but to me he was my Hodari. That man was something special. He showed me things that no other man in my life has ever shown me. The reason why our relationship was so strong was because not only was he my man, he was my best friend and he had all the quality that I ever wanted in a man. He was polite, tall, dark, and handsome. Something like one of those fairytale motherfuckers and he could work the hell out of that sausage that set between his legs. My mother tried to warn me about him though. She saw something in Hodari that I couldn't see. She would always say, "Child, that man means you no good. He is the devil," but I paid her no attention because she had something to say about every guy that came into my life. Even though she was right about the other guys, I knew that without a doubt she was wrong about Hodari. He was different. He had to be. He really made me feel special. No man has ever captured my heart like him. He had my mind, body, and soul. And in my mind if loving Hodari was wrong, I definitely didn't want to be right.

Dangerously in love is what I was and I really do hate he crossed a line that he was never supposed to cross. To hear another bitch moans escape from my bedroom and echo through my house sent me into a rage that I didn't know I had in me. I can honestly say that when I walked into our house, I never had any attentions on committing a 187 or an attempt murder for that matter. All I was trying to do was come home and cater to my man since they let me off work early that day, but instead of catering to him, I had to cater to my heart.

****

"Washington," you have a visit the CO yelled.

I was shocked that I had a visit. I have been lock up for exactly eight months and five days and not one of my so-called friends or family members attempted to come see me or even write me a letter. I was dealing with a lot of emotions while

7

locked up and I needed someone by my side. I jumped off my top bunk, slipped on my shoes, and dragged myself to the visiting room for the first time since I've been locked up with a perplex look on my face.

When I got into the visiting room, my eyes scanned it. I didn't see anyone that I knew. The visiting room was pack and noisy. I heard different conversation going on at once and babies crying. To say the least, it was music to my ear. I was tired of sitting in my cell staring at a wall.

"Table six," the CO said then pointed in the direction of the table.

I headed to table six only to be seated by myself and waiting on my visitor to arrive. My eyes surveyed the visiting room again, trying to see if anybody looked familiar from the streets and they didn't. Everyone looked so happy being with their love ones. I miss that type of love. As I continued to examine the visiting room, I noticed the bathroom door open and a very short petite woman exited. Her spirit felt familiar, but she didn't look familiar. I then turned my head in the direction of this one couple that had just hugged and kissed. They love looked so genuine and pure, but something drove me to turn my head back in the direction where the petite woman was. I wanted to know where this familiar feeling was coming from. There was really something about the woman that made me feel so warm in the inside. Before I got a chance to give her my attention there she was standing in my face with tears welling up in her eyes and a huge smile on her face.

"Momma," was all that I could get to escape my mouth. Tears slowly fell down my miserable looking face. I stood up from my seat and fell into her arms. I missed my mother so much. I was her only child and we were all each other had. For a brief second, I felt like an infant again being cradle by her. The love she gave off was so strong that she didn't even have to say a word. Then all of a sudden, I pulled away from her and gave her an allover glance. "Momma is everything okay with you?" I asked.

She broke eye contact with me then said, "Take a seat baby." We both took a seat at the small round table and sat across from each other. My eyes were glued to her every move. "Right now it's not about me, it's about you." That was just like my mother always putting others first, but I wasn't going for it this time. Something was wrong with my mom and she was going to tell me.

"Momma please tell me what's going on with you, you look so different." By the looks in her eyes I knew she was sick and have had to been sick for a long time. The tears in my eyes wouldn't stop flowing down my face. I was hurting inside and out. My mother was everything to me and if I didn't have her in my life, I'm not sure what I would do. I begged my mom for about five minutes before she gave in and told me what was wrong with her.

"Baby, momma is dying. The good lord is preparing for me to come home."

I couldn't come to grasp with what she was saying. I wasn't trying to hear that she was dying or even sick. I felt bad because I was in here and I couldn't be there for her.

"Momma, don't say that. You're not dying," I said as I dried my face. I tried my best to hold back my tears. I wanted to be strong for her. I couldn't let her see me weak even though I was dying inside right along with her.

"Baby, you know momma will never lie to you or even point you in the wrong direction, but I have accepted my fate and you will have to do the same. I am dying; I have cancer and it's very aggressive. This is why I haven't been to see you or write you. I been in and out of the hospital for months and I have been too weak to even pick up a pen, but God finally gave me enough strength to come and see my baby today. You know I would have never left you to fight this battle alone. I'm a little upset with you though because I told you that damn boy wasn't any good, but I'm not here to chastise you, I'm here to see what I can do to get my baby out of here.

"There is no getting out of here, this is my new home for the next sixty-five years," My mom almost passed out when she heard how much time the judicial system had given me for the first time. She had no clue that I was going to be caged away like an animal for that long. The first day trial started, she was there, but after that, she was a no show. Now I see why, it was all because of her sickness. I should have known there was a legitimate excuse for her absence.

I couldn't believe, I was only twenty-five and my life was over with before it even began. Her tears wouldn't stop rolling down her pie shaped face. I reach across the table to try to wipe her tears away, but one of the CO's told me to keep my hands to myself or my visit would be over. I wanted to smack the shit out of whoever made that stupid ass rule up of no touching once visitors and inmate are seated at the table. What they fell to realize is that this wasn't going to be any ordinary touch, my mom needed to be comfort because her heart was hurting from every angle. I hate to see my mother in so much pain and there wasn't anything I could do about it.

There were no more words exchanged between my mother and me for the next ten minutes, which seemed like an eternity. We both were letting the horrific news of each other marinate. This was a lot for us both to grasp, her illness and me being locked away for so long. We just stared at each other like this was going to be our last time laying eyes on one another so I broke the silence between us. I knew there were some things that she wanted to ask me, but she didn't want me to relive what I've been through. I had so much respect for my mother so it was only right that I told her everything from the beginning to the end. I cleared my throat and began to speak slow and precisely. "Mom, before I go into details of what have lead me up to this point, let me just say this, I know your heart is broken about what I've done, but he drove me to the point of no return. The devil was riding heavy on my back and has been for a long time when it came to Hodari, but I chose to over-look a lot of things that he was doing, but this was one thing I couldn't let him get away with." My mom grabbed my hand and told me I didn't have to say no more, but I continued. "There have been plenty of nights when I just wanted to die because I felt so alone in this place. I didn't have you to talk to. I thought you abandoned me, but now I see the reason why you didn't reach out. I tried to be angry with you for some many reasons, but I couldn't because the only thing you tried to do was protect me time and time again. I already asked God for forgiveness and now I'm asking you for yours for being a disobedient child. I need you to sympathize with me for a moment though and put yourself in my shoes because I'm sure you would have handled the situation the same way. I was blinded by love and there wasn't anything I could do about it. I had to learn on my own and I definitely learned the hard way. The crazy part about all this momma is that I will forever love that man. Call me crazy, stupid or whatever, but if you ever really love someone despite of what they do to you, your heart will continue to beat for them." My mother began to shed more tears of pain. "Momma, please don't shed no tears for me because I'm a big girl and I'll be alright, but before I tell you how this all started, let me just say one more thing. I don't want you to think I'm a sucker for love because I'm not. Even

13

though I'm in love with what me and Hodari had, he scarred me for life and I promise if I ever get out of here, just like I killed him I'm going to find and kill that bitch that helped him break my heart.

CHAPTER TWO

The Beginning

Jaliyah was standing at the altar looking magnificent in her cream Vera Wang wedding gown and Apollo was looking equally good. He was dressed in an all cream suit with a burnt orange vest to compliment her stylish, yet elegant look. Mariah must admit, her best friend of fourteen years was the most beautiful bride that she had ever seen. Jaliyah looked so happy standing next to the man of her dreams and it brought nothing, but tears of joy to her eyes. As Mariah stood next to her friend, she admired how gorgeous and perfect everything was set up around the church. There were beautiful flowers, white trees, and fake snowflakes everywhere. Jaliyah was having a white winter wedding in the middle of July. There had to be over a hundred guests at the wedding, and when Jaliyah made her way down the aisle to the altar, there wasn't a dry eye insight. This wedding must have cost them an arm and leg, but Jaliyah deserved to have the wedding of a lifetime. Mariah drew her attention back on the bride and groom and as they held hands, she heard the pastor say, "Is there anyone here today, who think these two should not be married, if so, speak now or forever hold your peace." There was complete silence in the room, which was music to everyone's ears. No one in the church was against them at all. They were all rooting for them because to find love at a young age was a blessing. Mariah smiled at the pastor who was on his way to continue with the ceremony, but what followed next nobody was expecting.

"Peace is not what I'll be holding," Tina ratchet ass spoke aloud.

Tina was a chick that Apollo was dating on and off for the last two years and Jaliyah has had plenty of run-ins with her. Mariah couldn't believe that Tina had the audacity to show up at Apollo and Jaliyah's wedding. Even though Tina didn't have an invitation to the wedding, she made it her business to put her ears to the street to find out the date and time of the event. She wasn't anything, but a cold hearted jealous bitch and once Mariah got close enough, she was going to fuck her straight up for messing up their wedding.

Tina glided from the back of the church to the front with all eyes glued on her. This crazy

16

bitch was dressed in a white wedding dress very similar to Jaliyah's. One of Tina's close friend worked at the same bridal store where Jaliyah got her wedding dress, this is why their dresses were so similar. "Apollo is my man and he will not be marrying this bitch," Tina said as she pointed in Jaliyah's direction. The people in the church mouth hit the floor. They were shocked and they couldn't believe what was happening right before their eyes. "Tell her Apollo, tell wifey how you came over my house last night and fucked me to the wee hours of the morning." Tina then directed her attention to Jaliyah, "You know I'm not telling a lie because he didn't sleep in your bed last night." The guests almost choked on their spit when Tina mentioned he didn't go home last night. The look in Tina's eyes were vicious and she was there to destroy this precious moment, and from the looks of it, she was about to accomplish her goal. Tina then drew her attention back on Apollo. "Tell her how you ate this pussy making me cum several times." She giggled while looking him dead in his eyes.

"You stupid bitch," Apollo squealed as his face carried a humiliating look. He quickly lunged in Tina's direction, but his best man, Hodari, grabbed him. He caught him when he was just inches away from her. Hodari knew if Apollo would have gotten to Tina, he was going to beat her to death in the Lord's house.

Tina's instinct caused her to jump back when Apollo lunged at her, but it didn't stop her from running off at the mouth. "Nigga don't get mad," Tina retorted. "I'm doing you a favor. I'm doing what your scary ass didn't have the guts to do." Apollo humiliating look turned into a blank stare. "You the one that texted me this morning saying you didn't want to marry the bitch and how you was making the biggest mistake of your life."

The silence in the room from the guest was unbelievable. You could hear a pen drop. Everyone just watched in awe. Tina continued to let everybody know how unfaithful Apollo had been to Jaliyah for the last four years. Most of the things Jaliyah knew about, but she was unaware that they were still messing around. Apollo was supposed to have stopped dealing with Tina a while ago, but apparently, he was still hitting the tramp.

Apollo couldn't stand to hear her voice another moment. He lunged at her again. This time Hodari wasn't able to stop him. His hands locked perfectly around her long thin neck. He choked her so hard that her eyes were bulging out. Tina tried to pry his hand from around her neck, but she was no match for his strength.

"You stupid bitch," Apollo repeated again.

For a minute or so, everybody just looked at the entertainment. Then the guests heard someone yell out, "Get him off her. He's going to kill that girl." Hodari suddenly broke out the daze he was in and he tried to pry Apollo's hands from around Tina's neck, but his hand wouldn't move. "Let her go man. She's not worth it," but Apollo wasn't trying to hear that shit. Tina had just messed up his life, and he wanted to end hers. The whole time this was taking place, Jaliyah just stood there in shock like everybody else. She didn't move nor blink. She was trying to get her mind to register what was going on.

As Apollo's hands got tighter and tighter around Tina's neck. He was determined to kill her in front of everybody. He didn't care about going to jail because the moment Tina opened her mouth, his life was over. "Die bitch," he shouted with so much hatred in his voice and Tina knew he meant every word of it.

Apollo heard the sweet sound of his mother's voice. She wasn't proud of her son's action, but she wasn't about to sit around and let him destroy his life over a woman. "Son, let her go, it's not worth it. She's not worth it."

For a moment his mother's cry wasn't being heard so she repeated herself again, "Please Apollo, let her go." His grip began to loosen from around her neck and Tina instantly dropped to the floor grasping for air.

Apollo was upset with Tina because she overstepped her boundaries. She had no business showing up at his wedding trying to destroy what him and Jaliyah had. Tina was just his side chick, not his woman and she knew that.

One would have thought that Tina have had enough and she would have gotten her ass off the floor and headed out the church, but she wasn't done yet. Once she caught her breath, she reached in her oversize purse that she had slung on her shoulder. She then looked Apollo straight in the eyes and screamed out, "I hate your bitch ass and since you put your hands on me, let me show you how real shit is about to get." Out of the purse came a hand full of papers. Everybody was wondering what could be on those papers, but their curiosity didn't last long. "Please take one and pass it down," Tina stated.

"Somebody escort this bitch out of here." Apollo yelled out, but nobody paid him any attention. What respect anybody ever had for him, left as soon as Tina opened her mouth.

"I don't need anybody to escort me out. Once my work is done here, I'll leave peacefully." Tina chimed a sinister smile and then winked her left eye.

Tina was tripping. Nobody could believe how she had managed to turn the wedding into a circus. As the paper floated around the church, Jaliyah continued to stand there in shock. Mariah walked over to Tina. She so badly wanted to knock her off her feet, but instead, she snatched a paper out of her hand because she wanted to see what all the oow's and ahh's was about. The whole stunt Tina pulled was unbelievable, but the paper took things to another level. Tina had taken a screen shot of the text message that Apollo had sent to her just moment before the wedding. She then emailed herself and printed it out. The message read *"Baby, I love you and just because I'm getting married, don't mean that I'm going to stop loving you. You will still have all the same privileges, good head, good dick, bills paid, and money in your pockets. This shit is just a piece of paper. I'm really just doing something to shut her mouth."* Mariah couldn't believe what she had just read and apparently, the guests couldn't either because there were loud whispers amongst the crowd. Mariah was disappointed in Apollo and just as much as Jaliyah had begun to hate him, she hated him too. How could he do her like this? He was supposed to love and cherish her for the rest of her life and now he turned her into damaged goods. The text message just didn't end there. He actually sent her two messages before the wedding and on that same sheet of paper there was a picture of Tina and Apollo hugging with his hands all on her ass and underneath the picture the text read, *"The real future Mr. & Mrs. Davis."*

Tina dream day had definitely turned into one of her worst nightmares. Personally, Mariah thought Tina came to the wedding on some hating shit, but she definitely backed up her story and there wasn't anything that Apollo could do at that point. Next time he will choose his hoes wisely; better yet, he just needs to keep his dick in his pants.

Tina walked up to Jaliyah as she stood at the altar by herself crying a river. Apollo had managed to disappear out the back door of the church as the papers were circulating around the room. Tina handed Jaliyah a paper with a smirk on her face, "Sorry boo-boo, these are your fiancée's words not mine. I never meant to hurt you, but he has been playing with your heart and mine for the last couple of years. I'm not going to lie, I love that man just as much as you love him, if not more, and there was no way I was going to let him walk down the aisle with you or any other bitch for that matter."

Jaliyah didn't say a word. She simply bald up her fist and knock the shit out of Tina. Tina went flying to the ground and Jaliyah stood over her stomping her with all of her might as her heels dug into her skin. Tina's tough ass tried to fight back, but she was no match for Jaliyah especially with all the built up hurt she was carrying. Nobody tried to stop Jaliyah from kicking Tina's ass. Everybody just watched as Jaliyah took all of her anger out on her and gave Tina everything she deserved. Jaliyah's beautiful dressed ripped in the process of her kicking Tina's ass and that made her even madder, so she started ripping Tina's dress off her. Then all of a sudden, Jaliyah stopped like something had clicked in her brain. She simply spat on Tina then walked away.

Mariah walked quickly behind Jaliyah. She grabbed her into her arms trying her best to comfort her, but she jerked away from Mariah, and ran into the three stall bathroom and locked it behind her. Mariah wasn't about to let her best friend go through this by herself so of course, she ran right behind her, but the door was locked. Mariah knocked on the door and pleaded with her friend until she finally let her in. Once in the bathroom, Mariah locked the door behind her.

"Everything will be alright. Fuck him. It's his loss not yours." Mariah said as she tried to give her some reassurance that she was a good woman.

Jaliyah looked up at Mariah with her makeup smeared and spoke softly through tears, "Everything will not be alright. I need him. Mariah, you will never understand how much I love that man. He was the best thing that ever walked into my life."

"Listen to yourself. You sound pathetic. You don't need him. You're strong, beautiful, and smart. Any man would be blessed to have you as his wife." It took a lot for Mariah to keep from saying, "I told you so," but Jaliyah's parade was already rained on and there was no need to make it soaking wet. Despite the things, Apollo did to hurt Jaliyah, deep down, he really did love her; he just had a funny way of showing it. In the beginning of their relationship, Mariah hated Apollo with a passion, but it wasn't about her, it was about Jaliyah's happiness so if Jaliyah chose to love him,

Mariah felt it was only right that she accepted him as well.

"I don't want any man. I want him," Jaliyah cried.

Their conversation was interrupted by a knock at the bathroom door. It was Apollo. He screamed from the opposite side of the door how sorry he was, but no words could possibly make up for the hurt that was in Jaliyah's heart. He fucked up big time, he knew it, and there was no coming back from this.

"Apollo, just go away. She doesn't need to hear your voice or see your face. Can't you see what you have done to her? Please, please just give her some space right now," Mariah said to Apollo through the locked door.

"I'm not trying to hear that shit Mariah, just open this door. She needs me." He stated while he jerked and pulled on the doorknob. "Baby I'm sorry. Please open the door. We can work this out," Apollo pleaded.

"Go to hell Apollo. As far as I'm concerned, you're dead to me." Jaliyah managed to muster up.

She didn't want to hear anything he had to say. He fucked up, not her. Apollo knocked on the door a couple more time before he got the picture and finally walked away.

"Jaliyah, I'm sorry this had to happen to you on your wedding day. If he still wanted to fuck other bitches he shouldn't have asked you for your hand in marriage."

"Where do I go on from here," she cried and Mariah gave her some Kleenex to dry her eyes. "I can't imagine my life without him. Six years, six fucking years are gone down the drain just like that. I forgave him plenty of times before, but this one I can't do." Briefly, there was a moment of silence. She just let her tears roll down her face. She had so much pain in her eyes. Her pain screamed betrayal. Of all the things someone could have done to hurt someone, this had to be the lowest. Mariah tried to think of the perfect words to say to help ease the pain, but before she could, Jaliyah continued to speak. "It hurt so bad, my heart is bleeding. How could he let his hoe humiliate me in front of my family and friends? This was supposed to be my day and she took that away from me."

Mariah held Jaliyah tightly in her arms and rocked her back and forth, as they sat on the bathroom floor. Jaliyah's tears soaked Mariah's bridesmaid dress and her foundation and mascara stained it. Mariah wished there was more she could do to take away her heartache. Mariah continued and tried to soothe Jaliyah with her words, but no matter what she said to her, this day will haunt her for the rest of her life.

CHAPTER THREE

It has been exactly two months since Jaliyah heart was broken in front of her friends and family. After that, she shut herself down to the world. I never imagined in a million years that she would shut me out of her life as well because we were best friends. I did my duty as a friend though, I reached out to her on several occasions, but each attempt I made was unanswered. After about two weeks of going by her house and calling her phone, I finally gave up. I had other shit going on in my life and I wasn't about to continue to waste my time trying to cater to a grown ass woman that didn't want to be catered to.

A couple of weeks passed before I finally heard from Jaliyah. I was delighted and pissed at the same time. I was delighted because she finally got her shit together and pissed that it took her so long to call me. There I was waiting patiently for her to walk in our favorite restaurant, Capital Grill so we could enjoy each other's company and a good meal. The waiter came over to my table and I told her to give me a couple more minutes because I was waiting on someone. The waiter simply smiled then walked away. I looked at my watch, *what's taking this girl so long*, I thought to myself, I was hoping she didn't stand me up.

As I waited patiently, I reached in my purse searching for my phone to make sure I didn't have a miss call from her. Indeed, there were no missed calls. I logged on to Facebook to kill some time and moments later after scrolling through my newsfeed, I received a friend request. I clicked the icon to see who wanted to be my friend and 'BoomIGotYourMan' was the person's name. I laughed and spoke softly to myself, "This hoe is crazy with this ridiculous ass name." I'm not going to lie though, her name definitely sparked my interest so I clicked on her picture and it took me to her profile. Her profile had limited information about her, but it did let me know that she was from Chicago. She was a very pretty girl, a red bone with high cheekbones, slanted eyes and a coconut smile. From her profile picture, she looked like a very well groomed girl. Her hair and makeup was on point, her small waist was complimented by an all-black fitted dress, and her feet were blessed with a pair of red bottoms. Next, I checked to see if we had any friends in common and we had none so I hit the delete button without any hesitation.

"Hey boo," was all I heard as Jaliyah's voice grabbed my attention away from my phone.

"OMG you look amazing," I said as I got up out of my seat and gave her a hug.

The person that was standing before me didn't look like the Jaliyah that I have known for the past fourteen years. She had given her image a makeover and I loved it. Jaliyah had cut her hair short that had a funky look to it and she had dyed it blonde. She even loss a good ten pound in all the right places. Jaliyah had always been a very pretty girl. Her skin tone was perfect and smooth. It reminded me of a caramelized honey latte from Starbucks. Standing like a stallion at 5'8, I could tell her confidence level elevated and I was happy about that after all she just went through.

She twirled around in a circle and said, "Tell me, do you like it?"

I couldn't do anything, but smile at my friend. She really did look amazing. We took a seat at the table and set there for an awkward moment just staring at each other. Even though she tried to paint a picture of being extremely happy, her eyes told a different story.

I broke the silence, "Girl I miss you so much. What have you been up to?"

Not giving me any eye contact after I asked the question, she simple answered, "Nothing much besides doing some soul searching."

"Good for you," I spoke with much excitement in my voice.

We chatted about everything that came to mind, and I made sure not to leave out the latest news about Hodari and I. "Guess what," I said to Jaliyah as my eyes lit up with joy.

A wide grin came across her face and she giggled between words, "What you do now?"

I began to giggle as well. "It's not what you think. Hodari and I have finally made plans to move in together. We are in the process of buying a house and we are about to start a family. Next week will be our first visit to the fertility clinic to see why I haven't been able to get pregnant."

"A baby," she spoke in more of a question rather than a statement. "You know that's some serious shit you're thinking about doing. A baby changes everything. I don't think you are ready for what comes along with being somebody's baby momma. You saw the shit I went through every time I got pregnant by Apollo. He would act stupid and as soon as I got rid of the little crumb, snatchers things between us got right back on track. Plus, he's a street nigga and street niggas

31

don't live long. You don't want your child to grow up without a father now do you?"

When I broke the news to Jaliyah, I wasn't expecting the reaction that she gave me. I was actually shocked, by her remarks. The bitch was definitely throwing shade and I wanted to know why.

"Damn, all I wanted was for you to be happy for me, but you giving me shade. I guess you can see the future because you basically just planned my baby's daddy funeral." I shook my head before I continued and pointed my finger in her direction. "You have some nerves of all people trying to give me some advice about a nigga. Did you forget the man you were about to marry was a hoe and a street nigga who treated you like shit? I didn't care if I hurt her feelings or not because she should have thought twice before she let those words roll off her tongue. "And to be honest, I wasn't telling you this to get your approval. I told you this so you could be happy for me, but I guess if you not happy, then you don't want anybody else to me happy. I see some shit just don't change when it comes to you.

Jaliyah saw the seriousness etched on my face. If she was anybody else, I would have reached across the table and smack the shit out of her, but I simply got up from the table so I could leave. I didn't come out for the negativity. I knew deep down inside Jaliyah was miserable and it was going to take a lot of time to get over what Apollo put her through, but I refused to sit around and let her take it out on me.

"Sit down Mariah, I apologize. You're my girl and if you are happy then I'm happy."

"Naw fuck that. You never had a problem with Hodari. Now all of a sudden you are insulting his character. What's really going on?"

"Just take a seat Mariah, I'm sorry," Jaliyah apologized again as she pointed at the seat.

I slowly took a seat back in my chair and watched her demeanor quickly change. Tears started to fall from her eyes. I had the slightest clue as to why she was crying. She definitely had me puzzled. I looked at her as if she was crazy. Hell, I should be the one crying because she was trying to crush my dreams. At that moment, I didn't care how she was feeling; I didn't care if she cried a river. She disrespected my man and I at the same damn time and I didn't like that one bit.

Jaliyah dried her eyes then began to speak. "I don't have anything against Hodari. He's my boy and you know that. It's just to the point that I see better for you. I don't want you to go through what I've been through. The different levels of hurt and the pain that seems like it will never go away. We both deserve better men other than these street niggas with fan clubs. My heart has been broken so many times and I don't want you to go through the same things that I have been through, but honestly I am happy for you."

I totally understood where she was coming from and I thanked her for trying to protect my heart, but she just went about it the wrong way. She needed to realize that my nigga is not like any man that she ever dated. He's not a liar or a cheater. He's perfect and the perfect man for me.

The waiter finally came back over and took our order and moments later, we both were back in good spirits. We chatted some more and made plans to take a trip to Dubai within the next couple of months. Our conversation was interrupted by the ring tone from her phone. She reached in her purse and retrieved her phone. When she looked at the name that flashed across the screen, there were mixed emotions wrote across her face as she looked back up at me before answering the call. She finally mouthed hello into the phone and it was a one-way conversation up until I heard her say, "I will be there in an hour."

For the first time, I noticed she still had the ring on that Apollo had given her. I wanted so badly to tell her to let it go so her heart could heal completely, but I left it alone.

"Now, where were we," she asked after she got off the phone.

"Girl, I forgot, but who was that on the phone." I asked being nosey.

"Nobody," she said as she smiled.

"Nobody, huh," I smiled back. I tried my best to overlook her ring, but it kept sparkling in my face. I couldn't hold it in any longer. My curiosity got the best of me. "Jaliyah, why are you still wearing the ring that Apollo gave you?"

She put her hand out in front of her and admired it. Blushing she began to speak, "Are you talking about this ring? If you are, you must be mistaken because this isn't the ring that Apollo gave me."

"Are you serious," I asked. I was shocked by her remarks. I was curious now more than ever as to what she had been doing these last couple of week we have not been in contact. Not waiting for her to reply I simply ask, "So if that not the ring Apollo gave you, who gave you that ring?"

Then she stated, "When the time is right, I will tell you, but until then just be happy for me."

35

CHAPTER FOUR

It was just a little after 7:00 p.m. when
Jaliyah arrived at the Westin hotel in Lombard.
She went straight to the front desk and gave her
name so she could get the key that was waiting for
her. The front desk clerk greeted her with an
attitude because she had plenty of run-ins with
Jaliyah about Apollo. Jaliyah didn't pay the girl
any mind though. She was at that hotel for one
reason and one reason only and in her book, she
was winning. Jaliyah politely grabbed the key,
smiled, and then strutted away toward the elevator.

Arriving at the room on the eighth floor,
Jaliyah heard sweet soothing music coming from
the other side of the door. She blushed, put her key
in the door and when she opened it, she couldn't
do anything, but blush even more. The room was
filled with I love you balloons and several dozen
of roses sat on a nearby table.

"Bae, where are you," Jaliyah yelled out
over the music.

"I'm in the bathroom. I'm just getting out
the shower."

"Hurry your ass up out of there. I told you I would be here in an hour. You should have been washed your stinking ass," Jaliyah said jokingly.

Jaliyah admired the nicely dimed room and then she walked over to the bed, set down, and admired the balloons and flowers again from a distance. *"This nigga is really showing out,"* she thought. Moments later, she heard the bathroom door open and out came her man with water glistening from the top portion of his body and a white towel covering the bottom half. She admired him while he walked toward her looking like Tarzan and smelling like a fresh bar of Dove soap. He didn't waste any time giving Jaliyah what he knew she needed and have been missing. He gently pushed her shoulders so she could fall back on the bed and he grabbed her by the waist, and pulled her so her butt could be at the edge of the bed. He then pulled her skirt up to her waist; his knees hit the floor one by one, and immediately starting licking on her kitty kat. Jaliyah knew exactly what her man liked so she came prepared with no panties on. After about a good five minutes of him licking her pussy there was a knock at the door.

"Don't stop. I'm almost there," Jaliyah said as she breathes heavily.

He acknowledged her request and kept pleasing her. Jaliyah moaned and groaned out of pure pleasure. The intensity of his tongue had her squirming. She was close to her climax when the knocks started again and it threw her off. She was pissed. She pulled his head from between her legs and said, "Apollo, let that bitch in."

Apollo got up with a wet face, opened the door, and in walked Tina dressed in a blue jean shirt, white jeans, and a pair of flat shoes. "I know y'all didn't start the party without me," Tina spoke sarcastically.

Jaliyah hopped off the bed, pulled down her skirt, and spoke with a smile on her face, "Listen here lil bitch you already know what it is."

"I got your bitch, bitch," Tina spoke sternly as she walked in Jaliyah's face.

"Calm down ladies," Apollo interjected as he pulled Tina by the waist.

"Naw fuck that; get your hands off of me because I'm tired of this trick's mouth. I think she forgot how things go around here. That's not just her dick, that's our dick," Tina stated as she pointed at Apollo's magic stick that drove them both crazy. "We all in this shit together; we are like one big happy family." Tina laughs after making her remark. "And furthermore, you two knew I was coming so if y'all wanted to fuck, suck or lick, y'all do that on y'all time not mine," Tina said feistily.

Jaliyah wanted to haul off and smack the shit out of Tina, but Jaliyah knew Tina was right. Jaliyah felt that since she had more time invested with Apollo, she had the upper hand, but Tina always had to give her a reality check. Jaliyah questioned herself repeatedly about her current situation, but knew love had the best of her and she was willing to do anything to have Apollo apart of her life.

****

Three days after the incident at the church, Apollo came to the house that he and Jaliyah shared and begging Jaliyah for her forgiveness. She didn't give in easily though. She told him she never wanted to see him again. She even wished death upon him, but after she saw him go in the bedroom to pack his clothes, she broke down and begged him not to go despite the embarrassment he caused her. Apollo was all she knew and she knew that as bad as she hated him at that moment, she couldn't bring herself to hating him for life. She was willing to do whatever it took to keep him in her life. Once Apollo discovered that, he knew he had Jaliyah right where he wanted her. He confessed to all his wrong doings, but then told her that he needed her and Tina in his life because they both completed him. She listened attentively as he went on about how they both added value to his life. Tina was shocked by his confession. Even though she felt like her chest had just caved in, she respected his honesty and fell into Apollo's love triangle. Jaliyah had so much time invested in Apollo that she didn't want to be with nobody else, but him. She had faith that in due time Apollo would change.

****

"Tina, enough is enough and I told you about your jealous ass ways. I didn't tell y'all to meet up with me for this. I wanted to meet up to show you both how much I appreciate you ladies and to discuss some business. Y'all see a nigga went out his way and bought roses and balloons."

"Nigga, does it look like I'm in high school? Fuck your roses and fuck your balloons and if you want to show me your appreciation show me some diamonds, better yet, show me your appreciation by cutting this bitch off," Jaliyah said as she pointed in Tina's direction.

Tina instantly charged at Jaliyah and got a hold of her hair, but couldn't get a good grip because of how short it was. Apollo grabbed Tina again and this time he smacked her. "Didn't I tell you to calm the fuck down? If you don't get it together, I just might take Jaliyah's advice and leave you the fuck alone. Now fuck showing appreciation, let's talk business and neither one of y'all say another word until asked."

Besides the music playing in the room, the room went silent. There were no words being spoken, not even from Apollo with the business he wanted to discuss. Tina stared at Apollo with hatred in her eyes because she was shocked he smacked her in front of Jaliyah. Apollo was in thinking mode; his mind was on money and Jaliyah soul burned with fire as she sat on the edge of the bed contemplating her next move. Jaliyah wanted so badly to pick something up and bust Tina upside her head. She was tired of Tina thinking that she ran shit and it was time she gave her a well-deserved ass kicking. Tina soul burned even more when she thought about how Tina ruined her wedding. She made a promise to herself that when the time was right, Tina will be dealt with accordingly.

Jaliyah eyes began to scan the room. They darted from one side of the room to the other looking for something that was going to cause some serious damage to Tina. Her eyes landed on the TV. She thought about picking it up and letting it land on her head, but she knew she would never be able to lift the television by herself so that was a no go. It wasn't much in the room that she could use so she smoothly reached in her purse that hung diagonally across her body without Apollo or Tina noticing her. Her hand landed on her box cutter. Jaliyah began to go into attack mode, but thought twice about stabbing Tina. She just wanted to cause her harm not end up in jail for a murder because the bitch wasn't worth it. Jaliyah then got off the bed and headed toward the table. She felt Apollo and Tina's eyes watching her. In a blink of an eye, Jaliyah grabbed the vase off the table, tossed the roses, and aimed the vase at Tina's head. Tina screamed out in pain and fell on the floor. Jaliyah ran over and started to kick and throw punches at Tina. Each punch that Tina felt was to her face and each kick was to her abdominal.

As Tina continued to scream out in pain, Apollo rushed over and grabbed Jaliyah putting her in a bear hug, but that didn't stop her, she gave Tina one good kick in her pussy. "Next time keep that nasty shit to yourself," Jaliyah yelled out.

Jaliyah managed to get one arm out of the bear hug and quickly went in her purse. She grabbed her box cutter and cut Apollo on his hand instantly causing him to let her go. "You bitch," Apollo yelled out in pain.

Holding her box cutter up for protection and waving it from side to side, she began to speak, "Nigga how dare you stop me from beating her ass after all she put me through. You need to be glad I'm not on top of you beating your ass as well for the part you played in breaking my heart. You are one lucky nigga though, you got a pass because I was in love with you, but her, real talk, she deserved that ass whooping and more. Every time I see the bitch, I'm going to kick her ass so Tina listen to me loud and clear you better watch your back. If I weren't so terrified of going to jail, I would have killed you with all this build up anger that's inside of me. Apollo you listen loud and clear as well, if you ever put your hands on me again, your mother will be burying your punk ass."

"Bitch is that a….."

Tina cut him off before he could finish his sentence. She knew exactly what he was trying to say. "No that wasn't a threat, it was a promise and one more thing; I'm done with this dysfunctional ass relationship. You and that bitch deserve each other," Jaliyah said still holding her box cutter in

her hand and heading out the door with her purse
still on her shoulder.

CHAPTER FIVE

"Hodari, where are you," I literally cried into my phone after receiving his voicemail for the fourth time. I sat in the parking lot of the Fertility Clinic of Illinois in Oakbrook Terrace and dialed his number again praying he answered and this time it went straight to voicemail. I was livid. I looked at my watch, time was now 2:35 p.m., and our appointment was in the next ten minutes. I began to hyperventilate. I felt dizzy, light headed and I started to sweat. I took several deep breaths trying to calm down, but that didn't work. It felt like I was going to die. I reached over, opened my glove compartment, and pulled out my brown paper bag. I did exactly what the doctor told me to do. He told me to breathe in and out of the bag because it causes me to re-inhale the carbon dioxide that I exhaled. After doing the breathing technique in the bag, I began to feel better. Just lately, I've started having these panic attacks and I think I know why.

I continued to call Hodari's phone and of course, the phone never rung, it kept going straight to voicemail. I glanced at my watch again and time was now 3:00 p.m. There were no words to describe how I was feeling at this point. All I did know was no man, no sperm, equals no baby and that had me really feeling some type of way. He told me he wanted this baby as much as me, but his actions are showing me something different. Hell, he is the one that talked me into going to the fertility clinic when I wanted to adopt. The more I thought about Hodari not showing up, the angrier I got. This is the third appointment he missed. How could he continue to do this to me? He better be kidnapped, six feet under or in jail because there is no way, I'm going to let him slide this time.

I finally started my car up and headed home. The ride back to my crib wasn't what I expected. My soul felt empty and gloomy, despite the beautiful weather we were having in the middle of October. Darkness was all around me and I didn't think I would be seeing the light anytime soon. I needed to drink my sorrows away and the first liquor store I saw I stopped at. Pulling up to Benny's liquor store, I quickly ran in. In a matter of minutes, I was walking out with a fifth of Patron in my hand. Feeling a little better knowing my soul was about to be tainted with Tequila, I sped through traffic so I could hurry up to get to my comfort zone.

Pulling up to my house, I rented from a good friend; I decided to sit in the car for a minute before I headed in. I had to give Hodari's phone another try. I dialed his number again and my heart lit up when I heard it ring. One ring, two rings, three rings, four rings and then, "Yo, this Hodari, you know what to do," the voicemail played in my ear.

"Fuck, fuck, fuck...what did I do to deserve this," I shouted out loud.

I got nervous as my mind-started racing. I thought about the text messages that I've been receiving from my ex-boyfriend for the last couple of days. Even though they were friendly text messages, how can I be so stupid to reply? My life is ruined. Hodari must have gone through my phone when I was sleep. Why didn't I delete those messages knowing how jealous Hodari can get? The last thing I wanted to do was piss him off with all the things we are trying to accomplish.

****

Hodari and I met a couple of years ago when he came to the law firm where I worked. He needed to be represented in a drug case that he was fighting. He came in dressed in a grey tailored made suit, but I could tell he was your typical drug dealer. Nothing got passed these eyes of mines because I grew up in the hood and I saw his kind every day so when he tried to give me small talk, I kept it short and simple.

"Excuse me beautiful; I noticed you're not wearing a ring on your finger. How is it that the man in your life can not put a ring on it," he articulated smoothly.

I looked at the clock that was on the wall behind my desk. "Mr. Adams will be with you shortly," I spoke a little agitated after turning back around.

"Thanks, but I didn't ask about Mr. Adams. Tell me about yourself. Tell me your likes and dislikes," Hodari smiled talking cocky.

"Listen...," I looked in the appointment book to get his name. "Mr. Edwards, I'm here to do a job, not have small talk with clients and plus, I know your kind and I'm not interested." I think I offended him because he walked away and didn't say another word.

The next day, I was called to the front of the office to sign for a delivery. I worked as a Paralegal so the day Hodari came for his appointment, I was relieving the secretary for her lunch break. I wasn't dating anyone at the time so I was definitely shocked to see a man standing there with a dozen of pink and white roses. I signed for the delivery and headed back to my desk. Upon sitting at my desk, I admired the roses and read the card that was attached. The card read, *you thought I was giving up that easy. Think again. Signed Mr. Edwards, but you can call me Hodari.* From that day forward, Hodari continued to sweep me off my feet.

Despite Hodari being burn in a car accident, I didn't let his physical appearance distract me from loving him. I was in love with his heart not his face and plus with the skin graphing they did, it covered his scars well. Hodari was a skinny dude. His body type would put you in the mind of Chris Rock. He stood five feet over me and I was only 5'5. His skin lacked the grace of smoothness and his eyes were distinctive, the color of the cherry you leave in your glass, yet his eyes would wonder from time to time. His tattoo on his neck gave him a thuggish appearance and it read "Money." He kept his haircut short in a fade that I love because of the grey streaks that ran through it. At the age of 26, he was wise beyond his years. He didn't let the streets raise him. He was book smart as well. He held a Bachelor's degree in Criminal Justice so for the most part he knew how to play both sides of the law.

****

Still sitting in my car, I quickly called Jaliyah because I needed someone to talk to. I really needed to get what I was feeling off my chest because Hodari had me pissed to the max. Tapping my finger on my steering wheel, I waited patiently as Jaliyah's phone rang in my ear. I got upset even more when her phone went to voicemail. Jaliyah was my best friend and I really needed her now more than ever because I felt like I was about to have a nervous breakdown.

Finally heading into my lonely house, I was greeted with boxes everywhere as I entered my domain. I was in the process of packing, it would just be a matter of days, possible weeks before Hodari, and I move in together. I was waiting patiently for the attorney to give me a call to come sign the closing papers. The house we bought was fit for a royal family, an all brick five-bedroom house, three-car garage with a long driveway, in Schaumburg.

Heading straight to the kitchen with my drink in hand, I grabbed my favorite shot glass out the cabinet that I got from sin city and sat at the kitchen table. I poured myself a shot of Patron and I thought about the bullshit Hodari pulled today, but couldn't help to wonder if he was alright. I finally lifted my glass and took a shot, another shot, and then another shot. Instantly, I started to feel the effects of the liquor. I began to feel all warm and cozy in the inside. My body and mind was taken to another place then all of a sudden the kitchen began to spin and my head started to hurt. I tried to get up, but almost fell so I sat back down. That's when my mind started to play tricks on me.

"Mariah, leave that nigga, he ain't shit," I spoke to myself having an outer body experience.

"You will be a fool if you leave him. He loves you."

"Girl, drop his ass like a fly. If he loved you, he would have been at your appointment today. Leave his ass and find a new man."

"Hodari is the best thing that ever happened to you."

"He don't want any kids, you are wasting your time."

It felt like I had the devil on one side of my shoulder and an Angel on the other. I quickly ran to the sink and threw some cold water on my face. Moments later, I felt the tears welling up in the corner of my eyes and once the first tear broke free, the rest followed in an unbroken stream. I blamed myself for Hodari not making our appointment. Why, I don't know, but I did. I hated myself and I felt like I was not good enough for him. I felt damaged. I wasn't even able to produce a child the natural way and I felt like I was running Hodari away. What is wrong with me? I questioned myself. Then I thought about my ex-boyfriend that gave me a sexually transmitted disease. It's all his fault that` I'm not able to give my man a child.

I headed over to the shelf that I had built on the side of my refrigerator and I reached under the breadbox and pulled my razor blade from underneath it. My childhood mentality took over me. I raised my left arm and placed it in front of me. Through my watery eyes, I stared at the marks that were still visible to me, even though I had Hordari's name covering it. I didn't want to harm myself, but for some reason, once that blade touched my skin, it made me feel good inside. I know it sounds crazy, but it really did take away my pain. My right hand met with my left wrist and I started slicing away. I didn't even wince. I didn't feel anything because my body was numbed. I sliced away until I heard Hodari's voice and by the time I looked up, blood was everywhere "Baby what you are doing. Stop it." I heard Hodari say.

CHAPTER SIX

Jaliyah got out of bed feeling the heavy bags underneath her eyes. These last couple of days has been sleepless without any communication from Apollo, she was mentally drained, but she knew she had to shake his worthless ass. She wished she could undergo a procedure that would erase him from her memory because she had begun to hate him and hate him with a passion. Within a matter of days, she went from loving him to hating him and he was going to pay for playing with her heart.

Walking over to her dresser, Jaliyah picked up her phone, glanced through her call log, and then shook her head. There were twenty-five missed calls. Twenty-four was from Apollo and one was from Mariah. "Fuck Mariah, her happy life and fuck Apollo and the bullshit that come along with him," she said out loud as she placed the phone back down on the dresser then headed to the living room. All Jaliyah wanted was for Apollo to leave her the fuck alone and stay far away from her as possible. She had it in her mind and heart that she was through with him for good. *He could be the next bitch problem*, she thought. It hurt her to the core that all the time she was loving him, he was loving someone else, and it was with the very same person he said was a non-motherfucking factor. Jaliyah thought she served a purpose in Apollo's life and as much as she wanted things to work out between them, he kept giving her a reason to walk away, and this time he gave her a good enough reason not to come back.

After placing the phone back on the dresser, Jaliyah headed to her living room and took a seat on her plush couch. She stared out of her big picture frame window and watched the clouds gather. They went from a perfect shade of light blue to a gravel-grey, the exact way she was feeling in the inside. She felt the temperature drop through the cracked window and it instantly starting pouring down raining. "Fuck, fuck, fuck...I'm not going to cry," she said out loud again talking to herself. Days like this she used to love. Cuddling weather is what Apollo used to call it. Every time it rained, he would wrap Jaliyah in his arms and whisper how much he loved and adored her, but all that ended the day he chose temptation over loyalty.

Knock....Knock...Knock...

There were a couple of light knocks at Jaliyah's door interrupting her train of thought.

Jaliyah just sat there as she continued to gaze out the window.

Knock...Knock...Knock...

The knocks started again, but this time they got louder and again she ignored the knocks because she didn't want to be bothered with anyone.

"Girl, open the motherfucking door. I know you hear me," Nu-Nu yelled from the opposite side of the door.

"Bitch go away, ain't nobody home," Jaliyah said while she dried her eyes and got off the couch heading back to her bedroom.

Jaliyah and Nu-Nu were first cousins and sisters. Jaliyah's mother Charlene and Nu-Nu's mother Darlene were twin sisters who couldn't stand each other because they both got pregnant by the same man. Charlene was married to Ronnie for ten years before she found out he was fucking her sister's brain out every chance he got. Once Darlene discovered that Charlene was pregnant, she stopped taking her birth control pills and in a matter of months, she became pregnant as well. Ronnie told her to get an abortion and she told him that as long as Charlene was walking around pregnant she would be too. He then threatened to beat the baby out of her. Darlene picked up, moved to Indiana with her best friend, and returned to Chicago with a bouncing baby girl a year later. She went straight to her sister's house and broke the news that Ronnie was indeed the father of her child as well. Charlene went crazy and beat the shit out of Darlene and when Ronnie walked in the house later on that night, she shot him leading him to an early grave. Charlene is now serving a life sentence, which left Darlene to raise the girls. Darlene didn't keep it a secret from the girls that they were both sisters and cousins. They accepted what was said to them at face value and took if for what it was. They had a choice though, to dwell on their parent's mistakes or make the best out of a fucked up situation, and they choice the latter. Only a select few knew the back-story behind Jaliyah and Nu-Nu and the rest of the world knew them as cousins.

As Jaliyah lay across her bed, she heard footsteps coming toward her room. She instantly opened her eyes, sat up, and yelled "Bitch, didn't I tell you wasn't nobody home and as a matter of fact give me back my key. I gave you that key for emergency purposes only."

"I don't know what your problem is, but you can keep your nasty ass attitude to yourself. I'm just checking on you like I do every morning or have you forgotten our routine, but you know what, fuck you and your attitude. I really just came over to get my purse I let you borrow. Now give me what is rightfully mine so I can take my black ass back across the hall to my apartment."

"Naw, please don't leave girl. I'm sorry Nu-Nu. I just have a lot on my mind," Jaliyah pleaded.

"Apology is accepted, but the next time you come at me with an attitude, I'm going to slap the shit out of you with no questions asked. Now what's bothering you," Nu-Nu asked.

Jaliyah just stared at the wall without saying a word. Then tears began to roll down her face. Nu-Nu walked closer to Jaliyah and gave her a hug. "Talk to me Jaliyah. What's going on? Did that bitch Mariah do something to you? If so, just say the word and I'll go beat her until she unrecognizable. You know how much I hate her."

"Naw, Mariah's cool, she hasn't done anything to me," Jaliyah replied.

"Listen sis, I can tell you have a lot going on. I've noticed it for a while, especially since the wedding. It's been writing all over your face and in your actions, but I didn't want to push the issue. I've been waiting patiently for you to open up. I know you like the back of my hands. We have the same blood running through our veins and when you hurt, I hurt too so just talk to me. Whenever you are ready to talk about it, I'm all ears," Nu-Nu said sincerely.

Jaliyah broke the brace that was between them. She stood up and paced her bedroom floor, then began to speak, "I put that on everything I love, I'm through fucking with that nigga. I hate Apollo ass. How stupid was I belittling myself by allowing him to fuck with me and another bitch at the same time,"

"Let me see if I understand you. Are you saying you still have been fucking with that no good, two timing ass nigga Apollo after what he's done to you and on top of that you accepted him along with another bitch? Is that what you saying because if so I'm not about to throw you a pity party. You have to be the stupidest bitch in the world. How could you allow him back in your life? Who is the bitch? Who is the bitch he got you accepting," Nu-Nu said as she stood there with her hand on her hips.

"It's Tina," Jaliyah blurted out embarrassed.

"Now I'm really convinced you are the stupidest motherfucker in the world," Nu-Nu said sounding disappointing at her sister.

"Nu-Nu, I'm not telling you this so you can criticize me. I'm telling you this because this was something that I really needed to get off my chest. The best thing you can do for me is be the ear that listens and the shoulder I need to lean on.

"Well, you told the wrong person. You know how I am. I'm going to call it how I see it and most definitely keep it one hundred with you. If you want sympathy for being a dumb bitch, you should have called the dumb bitch hotline or you should have called the dumb bitch Mariah, but I hope you are really through with him this time Jaliyah. I thought you were over him. So, is there really a new guy or was it a cover up so nobody would suspect you were still messing with Apollo," Nu-Nu inquired.

"Naw, I really do have someone new in my life, but I felt I had some unfinished business with Apollo. I'm serious this time when I say Apollo is the thing of the past. I just want to move forward and don't look back."

"So when are you going to let me meet the new guy. You have been dating him for the last couple of weeks and I need to size the nigga up to see if he's any good for you," Nu-Nu asked.

"Let me date him a little while longer before I bring him around the family so just be patient," Jaliyah said as her eyes diverted to the floor.

CHAPTER SEVEN

Waking up in the hospital had me feeling fucking stupid. How did I manage to fall back into my old ways? Slicing my wrist was the thing of the past, something I would do after I felt guilty for fucking my mother's boyfriend. At the age of nine, my life changed and that's because my mother fell back in love with her high school sweet heart who was a registered child molester. She had no clue of his past so only after dating him for six months she let him move in. In the beginning, we were one big happy family. I really enjoyed having James around; he was the first man that ever showed me love because I never got a chance to get to know my father. My father died before I exited the womb. James took us on vacations; we went out every weekend, only if it was just a trip to the local Baskin Robbins, he even took me to Walt Disney World, which is every kid's dream.

See, my mom wasn't anywhere near rich so vacations were the furthest thing from our vocabulary. Hell, she barely had money to pay the bills, but she managed to put a hot meal on the table every night. She made struggling look damn good with no complaints. She didn't let the money in her pocket define her so only after two years of loving my mom James began to love me just a little bit more. One day my mom went to the grocery store and he came in my room while I was playing house with my easy bake oven that he bought me. He told me I can be the mother and he could be the father. Not thinking anything negative was going to come out of the situation, I played along. Then all of a sudden James yelled out, "Let's have a pretend wedding. You can be the bride and I can be the groom." I smile because all I dreamt about was being somebody's wife once I was old enough. James hummed the traditional wedding song as he and I walked arm and arm marching to the tone of his voice as we exit my room. We marched down the hall, turned around, and ended right back at my bedroom. As soon as we got across the threshold, he said, "You can kiss the bride," and he stuck his wet tongue down my throat. It felt discussing. I pushed his face from mine and looked at him strangely. He looked at me and said, "You are now a woman. It's okay, I won't hurt you." I was scared and felt secure at the same time because James had never did anything to hurt me, but I knew him sticking his tongue down my throat was wrong. He saw the fear in my eyes so he combed his fingers through my silky hair trying to ease me. His touch made my light skin fluster. I began to turn red. He knew I was getting more uncomfortable by the second so he began to tell me how beautiful I am. "Mariah, you are one of the prettiest girls I ever laid eyes on, from your natural hair down to your beautiful skin. Trust me when I tell you that you are intriguing in every man's eye." I looked away; I felt embarrassed and walked over to my mirror that hung on my closet door. If James thought, I was beautiful I had to be. All these years I thought I was ugly because I looked different from my friends. I was a mutt. I was mixed with French, black and a whole lot of other bullshit. James continued with describing my beauty. The more he told me how beautiful I was, the more I began to see what he was seeing. James then walked up behind be in the mirror and lightly pushed my neck to the side as he bent down and kissed on it. Even though I was afraid, I welcomed his touch because I didn't stop him. He then began to fondle my little breast and then a tear escaped my eye. I was really hoping my mom would walk in the house at any given moment, but she didn't. He then led me by the hand to my twin size bed, removed my clothes, and then his, he told me not to be scared. Moments later, he entered his oversized dick in my small virgin vagina. I winced from the pain and frown when I saw all the blood on the bed.

James molesting me lasted for about seven months before he dropped dead of a heart attack. Before he died, he molested me every chance he got and even though my mom and I had a strong relationship, I was too afraid to tell her what James was doing to me because she loved him so much and I didn't want to steal her joy. This was the happiest I had ever seen my mom in my life and the saddest I had ever been in mine so shortly after he started molesting me, I became depressed. I knew I was depressed because one night, I caught an infomercial talking about depression and I had all the signs. I knew I was too fucking young to be depressed and to be having those type of problems, but the reality of it all was, I was and that's when I discovered the usage of a razor blade and the joy it bought to me.

****

"Babe how are you feeling," Hodari said as he exited the small bathroom that was attached to my room. I didn't even know he was there, but if I would have taken the time to scan my room, I would have noticed his lightweight jacket resting on the chair and his car keys resting on the nightstand on the side of my bed. I looked at Hodari and didn't say a word. I was too embarrassed to say anything because Hodari had no clue I was a cutter. I just stared into space. "Okay, I get it. You don't want to talk right now, but do know I'm here for you," he said as he took a seat on the side of me.

"Hodari, I love you. I'm sorry."

"I love you too baby, but you don't need to do things like this to get my attention."

Did this nigga think I did this to get his attention? Instead of slicing my wrist I should have been slicing his ass up for missing our fucking appointment. I didn't even try to correct him. I just let him think what he wanted to think, but I did bring up him missing our appointment.

"This is the third appointment that you have missed. I want this baby. I want to start a family and if you not ready just say so instead of standing me up and having me looking stupid.

"Listen Mariah, I do want a baby. Something came up and I'm sorry."

"Something came up my ass. I guess something came up all three times. I'm not stupid Hodari. Your actions are not matching the words that exit your mouth."

"Please don't make it seem like I'm missing these appointments intentionally. When is the next appointment," he asked.

"There is no next appointment," I said as tears began to well up in the corner of my eyes. I looked down at my wrist and noticed the bandage was soaked in blood. I pressed the nurse button so the nurse could come in to change my bandage.

"What do you mean there is no next appointment," Hodari asked innocently.

"Hodari, I'm done talking about it. Until you can show me differently, we can't have this discussion. In the meantime, in between time, I wish this nurse will hurry the fuck up," I said changing the subject.

The nurse arrived and did her job quickly. She then took my vitals and gave me some information pamphlet on suicide. I looked at her as if she was stupid. *Bitch I was not trying to kill myself,* I thought, but I so badly wanted to say it out loud. I kept my mouth closed though and let her continue with her spill because I knew if I tried to interrupt her, she would have written some medical shit down in my file that probably would have sent me to the psych ward.

Moments later the doctor came in and asked me a lot of stupid ass questions. I guess these motherfuckers really thought I was trying to kill myself. I simply acknowledged everything he was saying by nodding my head. I glanced over to the side of me and noticed Hodari being very attentive. After the doctor got all of his questions answered, he smiled and said, "I'm free to go. The nurse will be back in shortly with my discharge papers."

Hodari and I finally left the hospital. I looked at my cell phone for the first time and I didn't realize that I was in the hospital for all those hours. I was just glad that Hodari walked in my house the time that he did because if not I would have kept slicing my wrist and I'm sure I would have been dead even though killing myself wasn't my intention. I had so much going on in my head when it came to having a baby, but I'm going to let that be the thing of the past until Hodari can show me different.

Finally pulling up to my crib, I got out the car and Hodari wasn't too far behind. He grabbed my arm and stopped me in my tracks. I turned around and looked at him and he apologized to me again.

"Baby I'm sorry. I really want you to forgive me."

"I told you at the hospital that I forgave you so please drop the subject," I said then broke away from his grip.

As I continued to walk toward my house, I realized I was mentally drained from this baby shit. My focus now was packing the rest of my things and waiting on the call from my realtor. Upon Hodari and me entering the house, we shook our heads at the same time as our eyes landed on all the boxes.

"Baby, I got this," Hodari said. "Go lie down and get you some rest."

I didn't interject to what he was saying that was the least he could do so I went in my room to relax. Not even twenty minutes later, I heard Hodari's phone ringing. He never put his phone on vibrate because he said he hated the vibration feeling when the phone be in his pocket. Hearing his phone wasn't unusual for me because it ranged all the damn time. What was unusual was the fact the phone had a special ring tone. Any other time the phone would ring to one of those generic ring tones that was installed in the phone, but this ring had some song playing. I couldn't make the song out, but I so badly wanted to get out my bed and ask him who the fuck was that calling him.

CHAPTER EIGHT

"Nigga, I know you see me calling your ass. Call me back as soon as you get this message." Nu-Nu said as she left Hodari a voicemail.

Jaliyah gave her sister a dirty look then said, "I thought you were done fucking with him.

"I was done fucking with him, but apparently he wasn't done with me. After he kicked me down those stairs and made me have a miscarriage five months ago, I really was trying my best to write his ass off. I even threatened to tell his bitch about us if he didn't stay away from me, but that didn't work and Lord knows I wanted that baby by him so bad to rub in his bitch face because she can't have kids and on top of that, I would have been set for life. Oh, just a FYI, Hodari don't love that bitch like you think he do. That nigga loves me because if he didn't, he would have stayed away from me to protect his relationship at all cost," Nu-Nu replied.

"Nu-Nu, remember how you told me I was the stupidest bitch in the world, guess what you just made the stupid bitch list. Hodari loves you and every other bitch he sticks his dick in," Jaliyah said with a serious look on her face.

"Fuck you Jaliyah,"

"Naw, fuck you Nu-Nu, you can dish shit out, but you can't take it. All I'm going to say is be careful."

"Be careful my ass, that's my dick. You need to be telling that to your girl because I'm definitely coming for her life.

****

Nu-Nu and Hodari had been messing around for the past year and a half and have been having the perfect relationship despite him having a woman up until she got pregnant. Once Hodari found out she was pregnant, that's when things changed between them. Hodari stressed repeatedly how he wasn't ready to be a father so he made sure that every time it was time for her to take her birth control pills, he was around to monitor her. He basically hand fed her the pills himself. Condoms wasn't an option for him when it came to Nu-Nu, he loved raw dogging her. He loved the way her pussy felt without the rubber. Despite the precaution that Hodari tried to take, Nu-Nu had other plans for him. She played right along with him making him feel like he was in total control.

She popped her pills faithful, but it wasn't birth control pills that she was popping it was vitamins.

Coming up on their one year anniversary of being in a relationship that's when Nu-Nu delivered the news to Hodari that she was four month's pregnant and he didn't take it well. He instantly went in his pocket and peeled off $1,000, not knowing how much it would cost for an abortion and tried giving it to her, but she refused to take the money. Not taking the money pissed Hodari off even more. Nu-Nu knew that he didn't want kids by her, but she thought if the baby was already in her stomach developing, it would have changed his mind. After that they had a huge argument and one thing led to another with Nu-Nu slapping the shit out of Hodari and him kicking her down a flight of stairs.

Nu-Nu met Hodari at a cookout that Jaliyah threw at Columbus Park for Apollo's birthday and when Hodari laid eyes on Nu-Nu, he instantly was drawn to her and it wasn't because of her looks. She wasn't drop dead gorgeous. Hell, she wasn't even average. Actually, she was below his standards, but what drew him in was her oversize breasts. Hodari was a tittie man. He loved women with big breast and that was one thing Mariah was lacking.

Nu-Nu was the average height for a woman. She stood 5'5 and her sculpted figure was way more than twine-thin. She was thick as hell with a flat ass and wide hips. Her round shaped, ochreous hue colored face was accompanied by a couple of dark spots that wouldn't go away, but when she broke into a smile her charming, oyster-white teeth lit up the room.

"Hey pretty lady," Hodari said as he grabbed Nu-Nu's attention away from her cell phone that was in her hand.

Nu-Nu turned around and her eyes landed on Hodari. "Heyyy, you are Apollo's friend, Hodari right."

"Yep, that's me and you are Jaliyah's cousin Nu-Nu right."

"Yep, that be me," and they laughed in unison.

"Can I get you a drink?"

"No, I'm good. I'm not a drinker," Nu-Nu said.

"A drink isn't going to kill you. Have a drink with me with your sexy ass," Hodari said flirtatiously."

Nu-Nu blushed then said, "Where your girl at? I'm sure she somewhere lurking. I don't want any trouble."

"Ma, listen, first off you worried about the wrong thing, and secondly I would never put you in harm's way." Truth of the matter was Mariah was at home in the bed sick.

Nu-Nu smiled and followed behind Hodari as they headed to his car to get his drink. Instead of them joining back with the festivities with everyone else, they got in his car, pulled off, and enjoyed their drink. Four cups later Nu-Nu was drunk and Hodari was tipsy. Instead of them driving around, Hodari pulled up to the Ambiance Inn & Suites, checked in and they fucked on and off for the next four hours.

After Hodari dropped Nu-Nu off back at the cookout, his plan was to never see her again sexually. All he wanted was a quick fuck because lately he's been tired of fucking the same pussy, but the more he thought about how good her pussy was he knew that he couldn't stay away from her so from that day forward they stayed in each other lives.

****

After Jaliyah and Nu-Nu's brief conversation, Nu-Nu left and headed back to her apartment. She called Hodari's phone again and this time he answered. "What's up," he said as he whispered into the phone.

"Nigga don't what's up me. You told me you had to make a quick run and you would be back in an hour so where are you?" Nu-Nu asked.

"How many times do I have to tell you not to question me? I'm a grown ass man and on top of that I'm not your man so where I am don't matter."

"But you want to fuck me every chance you get like you're my man," Nu-Nu said with an attitude.

"Listen, I'm at my girl's crib, I will hit you back later," Hodari replied to get under her skin for questioning him, but it was the truth.

"What the fuck you doing over there, you're supposed to be here with me. I'm tired of playing second to that skinny Ethiopian looking ass bitch of yours. We have been at this for too long. It's time you make a choice on who you want to be with."

"Choice is made, goodbye Nu-Nu since you don't know how to play your position." Hodari said then ended the call.

Hodari had a lot on his mind, but Mariah was his main focus. He didn't have time for Nu-Nu bitching and moaning and when he saw her, he was going to kick her ass and put her in her place.

All Nu-Nu had to do was fall back and play the role that was given to her, but she wanted more than what Hodari was willing to give. In Nu-Nu's heart she knew she didn't have a chance at being Hodari's woman, but she was going to try everything in her power to prove to him that she was worthy.

"I know this nigga didn't hang the phone up on me," Nu-Nu said out loud as she looked at her phone.

Nu-Nu tossed her phone on the couch and paced back and forth in her living room. She hated when Hodari hung the phone up on her. She have told him time and time again that if he ever hung the phone up on her again that he would pay big time and this time she meant it. Hodari had her pissed to the max and every time he pissed her off, she got pissed with herself for not leaving him when he kicked her down the stairs. Hodari didn't care about her when she was pregnant with their unborn child and he definitely didn't care about her now especially the way she wanted him to. She demanded the highest respect from Hodari and that was something that he wasn't willing to give because his heart already belongs to somebody else.

Nu-Nu continued to pace her wood floor for a few more minutes before deciding to head to her bedroom to get dressed. She took off her Victoria Secrets Pink gown and tossed it in the dirty clothes hamper that set on the side of her dresser. She then open up one of her dresser drawers and grabbed a pair of leggings and a long shirt that would cover her ass and she put that on. Her eyes zoomed around her room until they landed on her all black Nikes. She grabbed those from the foot of her bed, threw them on, and laced them up quickly.

At this point, Nu-Nu had one thing on her mind and that was to go to Mariah's house and tell her about her man. Nu-Nu knew exactly where Mariah lived because she once had a tracker on Hodari's IPhone and tracked him there plenty of times. As long as he was tracked to Mariah house, she was cool, but if he was tracked to any other female house, it would have been a major problem. As Nu-Nu reached in her closet to grab her purse, she heard a knock at her front door. She quickly grabbed her purse, threw it on her shoulder, and headed toward the front door.

"Who is it she yelled as she got closer to the door."

"Bitch, it's me open up," Jaliyah said.

Nu-Nu blew out frustrated air and opened the door. "Make it fast because I have to go."

Jaliyah stepped in the house and closed the door behind her. "Where you going this early in the morning," Jaliyah asked puzzled because she knew her sister was a night owl and she normally slept throughout the day.

"To your friend Mariah's house to tell her about her man," Nu-Nu said.

"Girl sit your ass down somewhere, you straight tripping. When you first told me, you fucked Hodari, I told you to stay far away from him and not to do it again, but you didn't listen. Now, your lil feelings are wrapped around him. You knew what you were dealing with and you knew he had a woman from the jump. If you were any other bitch, I would have told Mariah about you and Hodari, but since you my sister, I kept my mouth closed. I'm going to tell you this one last time, stay away from Hodari."

"I love Hodari and Hodari loves me so ain't no staying away," Nu-Nu said.

"There you go with that stupid shit again, but since Hodari loves you so much, did he tell you that him and Mariah just bought a house together and plan on starting a family. I'm sure that's one of the main reason he kicked your ass

76

down those stairs. He don't want no baby by his side hoe only the main hoe get those privileges."

The words that escaped Jaliyah mouth cut through Nu-Nu like a sharp knife. "Fuck you and the lies you telling me with your miserable ass. You just need to face the fact that Hodari don't love your friend anymore and since you or Hodari don't have the heart to tell her what's really going on, I'm going to be the one to do it," Nu-Nu said then pushed passed Jaliyah leaving her standing in her crib.

CHAPTER NINE

Hearing Hodari' in the living room on the phone had me feeling some type of way, but I shook that feeling very quick because I trusted him. He never gave me a reason not to trust him. I never had a run in with any chick about him or any calls placed to my phone so yes, it's safe to say I trust my man and plus if he was cheating, I know he didn't have enough balls to talk to a female on the phone when I was in the next room.

Finally closing my eyes, I did exactly what Hodari told me to do and that was to get some rest. As I was dozing off, I heard my front door slam shut and my cell phone vibrated on my dresser at the same time. Ignoring the vibration of my phone, I quickly jumped up out my bed and ran downstairs to catch Hodari to see where he was going, but by the time I made it, he had already gotten into his car and was pulling out the driveway.

Heading back up to my bedroom, I went straight to my dresser to grab my phone. I thought about calling Hodari to see where he was going, but dismissed that thought as quickly as it jumped into my head because I was still rather pissed with him for not showing up for our appointment with the fertility doctor. When I looked at my phone, I had missed a call from my realtor. I called her back and what she had to say was good news to my ears. She told me that I needed to come sign the closing papers first chance I get. With me going to the hospital for slicing my wrist all I wanted to do was rest for the remainder of the week so I told her I would come to her office Monday after work.

Getting the good news about the house had me feeling good. I'm one-step closer to living out my dream with the man of my life. Hodari and I never discussed marriage, but that will be the next thing I bring up because buying a house and trying to conceive with a man that's not my husband wasn't a part of my dream. Having a husband is all I dream about since I was a kid. I wanted to have something that my mother never had or any other woman in our family. It's one thing to share love with someone, but to share love with your husband was a whole other level.

Standing on the side of my bed, with my phone still in my hand, I thought on how I wanted to deliver the good news to Hodari. I didn't know if I wanted to tell him over a nice candle light dinner or if I wanted to simply call him. I thought on it for about five minutes before I decided to just text him. I didn't want to deal with waiting all day for him to come back to my crib or take the chance of him not answering the phone and me getting upset. I took the safest way I could think of and I knew he would receive my message if he were busy or not.

I sat down on my bed and began to text. *"Bae, I just spoke with the realtor and she told me all I have to do is come sign the closing papers and we can get the keys. Baby we are now a homeowner."* I ended the text with several smiley kissy face emoji's.

Hodari texted back immediately with three words, *"I love you."*

With those three words and the great news I just received, I forgot all about being mad at Hodari. I walked to the kitchen and poured myself a glass of wine to do a little celebration, then headed back to my room to get some much-needed rest.

****

Monday morning rolled around quicker than I imagined. I thought I was going to be dog-tired, but the workday was going by smoother than I thought even though Hodari and I did a lot of celebrating and love making. That past weekend was all about us. He powered his phone off for the weekend and I did the same. After giving him the great news about the house, two hours later he returned with roses and a small gift box. My eyes lit up when I saw the black box. I was hoping that it was a size six, 5-karat diamond ring in there. When he approached me, I was sitting on my sectional couch, he got down on a bended knee, and he confessed how much I meant to him. My heart started to beat a little faster and I began to tremble. At that moment I knew he was about to ask me could he change my last name. When Hodari opened the box, my eyes stared at a beautiful diamond necklace. Even though I wanted a ring bad as hell, I admired the necklace and his great taste. I had never seen a necklace like that before a day in my life. I'm sure it cost him an arm and leg, but I knew I was worth that and more. It was just a matter of time before he asked me to be his wife.

****

Wrapping things up at work, I glanced at the clock and smiled because I only had thirty more minutes before it was time for me to clock out. I walked a couple of files over to the file clerk and had her to file them away for me. I then walked in my boss' office to see if she had anything important that needed to be done before I left for the day and she didn't. I headed back to my desk, straighten it up and then I grabbed my gym shoes from underneath it. I slid off my heels and replaced them with my Nikes.

"You've got mail," the computer announced as the little e-mail icon popped up in the bottom right corner of my computer screen. *Damn, I only have ten minutes left before I clock out,* I thought to myself as I slid on my last gym shoe.

I hated when Mrs. Walker pulled this bullshit at the very last minute. I just left out her office asking her if she had any last minute work for me and she said no so I don't know why she e-mailing me now. All I wanted to do was get out this depressing ass law firm just like she did. She wanted to run out so she could get to her big ass house, her husband, and kids and all I wanted to do was go meet my realtor so someday I can be like her. I knew my day was coming soon because with prayer anything is possible. Trying my best to ignore the e-mail icon at the bottom of my screen, I thought about the shit I had to do and there was no way in the world I was staying passed 5:30p.m.

I sat at my desk trying to look busy for the next couple of minutes and then I started gathering all of my things so I could get the hell up out of there. Right when I was about to shut my computer down, there was that familiar voice again "you've got mail." My curiosity got the best of me after I glanced up from my computer screen and looked in the direction of Mrs. Walker's office, only to see her lights cut off. I clicked on the icon and up popped my e-mail. I wasn't familiar with the name of the person that sent the message. For all I know it was somebody trying to send my computer a virus, but when I noticed Hodari's name as the subject in black bold capitalized letters, curiosity killed the cat. A big lump formed in my throat as my eyes read the email.

Good Evening Ladies, "What the fuck is really going on," I shouted out as I noticed I wasn't the only one this chick sent this message to.

My name is…well, none of that matters. I'm coming to y'all because I need to get to the bottom of some things. I've been getting conflicting stories about my man. I hear that he is engaged to one or either both of you, but that really can't be possible because he's engaged to me. I've been seeing Bae Bae, yea that's what I call him for a lil over four years now, and lately I've started to get the strangest feeling that I am not the only one. Mainly because he's been staying out to the wee hours of the mornings and you two bitches names are starting to ring bells. Excuse my French, but put yourself in my position if you would have found out the man you've been faithful to, the man you planned on having kids with, and the man you planned on spending the rest of your life with has been living a triple life. I'm sure you ladies understand my frustration, but if you don't, just put yourself in my shoes for a minute. Not sure if what I'm hearing is true, but Mariah, I've heard that you and Hodari are due to marry sometime next year. Keisha, you two are supposed to get married sometime this year. I was told that since Keisha is the mother of his two kids that I should just walk away from the situation because they have history and he's not going anywhere. Fuck naw, I'm not walking away, he's my man. He belongs to me. I'm sitting here laughing because Hodari and I are expected to be married this year as well. I'm not sure which story is true or if both are true, but this is why I'm sending this e-mail to get to the bottom of this so we can nip this shit in the bud. I'm a woman before I'm anything and I'm sorry if there is some type of misunderstanding and y'all don't know my man so please do accept my apology for bothering you two, but if there is some truth to this story, I'll be waiting patiently for a response. Better yet, y'all have one or two choices. We can handle this like ladies and y'all walk away peacefully or we can handle this like hood bitches. I'll just beat both of y'all ass and then force y'all to walk away. I normally don't fight over dick, but in this case there is an exception so do y'all self a favor and pick what's behind door number one and there will be no problems.

Signing,
The Future Mrs. Edwards

I continued to stare at the computer screen as each letter jumped out at me. I re-read the e-mail to make sure my eyes wasn't deceiving me. I wanted so badly to pick up the phone to call Hodari, but this was a situation that needed to be dealt with face to face. I needed to see his body language because the moment he started to rub his hand together, then brush his hand across his goat-tee I knew he was lying.

It felt like time had stopped as I continued to sit at my desk. Going to sign those closing papers was the furthest thing from my mind. I was discombobulated. My thought process was all over the place. Killing Hodari was definitely on my mind. I wanted to rip his heart out of his chest because my heart was just been ripped out of mine. I even wanted to Lorena Bobbitt his ass. I never had any altercations with a woman about Hodari so I figured this had to be some type of mistake, but then I thought of how stupid that would have been of me to think that. How in the hell did this bitch know my e-mail address? It didn't take me long to figure it out. I quickly answered my own question and all I could do was shake my head. Hodari and I wanted to go out of town for the weekend, nowhere far, just to Wisconsin Dells, but he needed permission from his parole officer so I was going to type him up a letter using my job's letterhead. I texted him my e-mail address so he could forward me the guidelines of asking permission to travel out of town so I'm more than sure this is how the bitch got my e-mail address. He had to be laid up with her and she went through his phone because his phone never leaves his side. I couldn't believe this shit. I wasn't going to deal with another cheating ass man. I couldn't relive my past relationship of being cheating on, used and abused. My body began to quiver because he has shown and proven to me up to this point that he was different. He has been loyal to me so I do not understand why after three years this shit was happening. Just as soon as we get in our glow, some bitch had to come and dim the light.

I couldn't put all the blame on the woman because Hodari is our common denominator. How could he do this shit to me after all I've been through? I kept my past no secret so he knew all about my heartaches and pains, and he promised me that he would never hurt me as they did. He promised to protect my feelings and heart no matter what, but look at what he did. How foolish was I to believe him when he said he wouldn't hurt me? All these men are alike, some are just a little smoother than others, but all their ass cheat and on top of that, he could be cheating on me with two bitches. I shook my head again in total disbelief as the tears finally made their way down my face. I tried to control them, but they wouldn't stop. As I continued to think, I began to upset myself even more when I realized that there was a strong possibility that I'm not the main bitch. Hodari and I didn't live together so there is no telling where he's laying his head when he's not at my house. Before I got a chance to fully register everything that was going on, I heard that familiar voice again, "you've got mail." My heart couldn't take another e-mail, but I had to read what was going on with the man that I say I love. My heart instantly dropped to my feet as I began to read Keisha's response to the e-mail.

This has to be some type of joke right? Hodari is my man. We have a family together. After 15yrs of being together, I'm not sure where you two fit in so to answer your question it is true that me and him are getting married this year, yes, July 24th *to be exact. How can any of you claim him as y'all man when he lives with me. Silly women you are. There's no need for me to elaborate any further just know he's my man, my fiancée' and the father of my two kids and I'm the real future Mrs. Edwards. If you have any questions contact me at 773-555-1947.*

After reading Keisha's response reality set in real quick. A bitch thought she was about to flat-line. I was no longer living this fairytale ass life. Hodari was no longer my knight in shining armor. I quickly picked up my cell phone and punched in Keisha's number. The phone only rung once before I heard the recorded person say, "State your name after the beep." That wasn't even her real number. She gave me a Google voice number. I stated my name and the call rang a couple of times before my call went to voicemail. In a way, I was glad it did go to voicemail. I wasn't thinking

88

rationally. My beef wasn't with her it was with Hodari.

I swear I was so disgusted with that nigga. He was really living a triple life, but July 24th played over and over in my head. Hodari is a fucking trip. July 24th is the day I went to the clinic and found out my chances of having kids was slim to none. How dare he start a beautiful beginning with someone on the same date that my life technically ended? In a split second, what I thought was a happy life has been flipped upside down. There were no words to describe what I was feeling at that moment. I began to rock back and forth in my chair. My eyes turned blood shot red without me shedding another tear. I was too hurt to continue to cry. I needed to find the underlying cause of this fast. Keisha said that Hodari lived with her and the other girl said he lived with her and to my knowledge; he stays in his mother's basement. I've spend plenty of nights at his crib, but how can any woman that clam their man lives with them allow him to spend the night out. There is definitely some foolery going on. I grabbed my purse, shut down my computer and rushed out the office, but before I did that, I made sure I printed that e-mail out so Hodari could see for himself what was going on.

CHAPTER TEN

Leaving out her house, all Nu-Nu wanted to do was fuck Hodari up. How dare he kill her child just to start a family with another woman? Thinking about what Hodari had done to her, made her want to hunt him down like a deer and chop his ass up, but hurting him would only hurt her chancing at having him love her more. For now, she was going to play it smooth with him. When the time was right, she was going to strike. The shit that Nu-Nu had up her sleeve Hodari will never see coming. With her heart crushed and a sinister smirk plastered on her face, Nu-Nu headed to her car, but instead of paying a visit to Mariah's house like she planned, she headed to her mother's house because she needed someone to vent to. She knew she could talk to her mother without being judged unlike Jaliyah.

"And what do I owe the pleasure," Darlene stated as her eyes landed on her daughter.

"It took your ass long enough," Nu-Nu said with an attitude as she stood on the opposite side of the door.

"You better be glad I answered this motherfucker. I was knocked out sleep and here you come disturbing my beauty rest."

Nu-Nu push passed her mother as she blocked the doorway. "Momma don't start with your bullshit today because I don't want to hear it."

Walking into Darlene's studio apartment, Nu-Nu was on the verge of throwing up. It smelled like sex. It smelled like her mom had been fucking all day and night while on her period. The smell of Darlene's house didn't match the mood of the apartment. The house was spick and span clean and you could have eaten off the floor if it wasn't for the smell. Nu-Nu put her hand over her nose and headed straight to the bathroom to get the air-freshener and instantly started spraying."

"What you trying to do, kill a bitch? Open up some damn windows," Darlene yelled.

"Naw, you're the one trying to kill a bitch with this fish smelling ass house of yours."

"Well die then and why are you over here anyway. What do you want? I'm still mad with you for not coming back the other day," Darlene said as she took a seat on her black leather couch.

Letting up two windows to get some fresh air circulating through the house, Nu-Nu replied,

"Well, get over it because I need some motherly advice."

"Before you get started, I need to know if you have some money because I'm broke. I'm hungry and there ain't any damn food in this house to eat."

Nu-Nu began to laugh then took a seat next to her mom. "Weren't you the same person that told me that as long as a woman have a pussy she should never go broke and the last time I checked not only do you have a pussy, you told me it was made of gold."

"You are a sarcastic li'l heffa I see."

Not feeding into Darlene's bullshit any longer, Nu-Nu began to get serious. "Mom, I got shit going on and I've been having these thoughts about this person for a while. I know what I'm thinking is wrong, but it would make me happy."

"Girl, stop beating around the bush and tell me what's going on."

"I want Mariah dead," Nu-Nu said not holding back.

"Who the fuck is Mariah," her mother said puzzled.

"The li'l bitch who man I'm fucking."

"Let me ask you this, do you love him and you can't see yourself living without him," her mother asked sincerely.

"Yes, I love him and no I can't see myself living without him."

Going on to the next question, her mother ask, "Do he love you?"

Nu-Nu eyes lit up. "Hell yea he loves me," Nu-Nu replied even though she knew it wasn't the truth. The only thing Hodari loved when it came to Nu-Nu was the convenience that she provided.

"Well kill the bitch," Darlene said with a smile upon her face.

Darlene and Nu-Nu had a strange relationship. They acted more like sisters than mother and daughter. For some reason, Darlene felt like she owed her daughter because she chose the wrong man to produce a love child with. Her daughter missed out on being daddy's little girl. She missed going to the father and daughter dance and spending those special holidays, such as birthdays, Christmas, and Thanksgiving with her father. She missed everything that a girl should have when it came to her father, but most importantly, she missed out getting to know that man that her mother once loved.

"I knew you would understand," Nu-Nu said as she went in her purse and grabbed two small pieces of alumni foils and placed them on the table. She got off the couch, headed to the kitchen, and grabbed two spoons and a small cup of water. Her mother face was lit up like a Christmas tree when she returned. Darlene then got up and went to her room and when she returned, she had two clean needles. Darlene was a diabetic so she had fresh needles handy all the time. Nu-Nu grabbed her mother box of Newport that sat on the table and grabbed two cigarettes out. She bit the butts off the cigarettes, and grabbed the cotton from the inside and placed it on the table. As if on cue, they both went for a piece of alumni foil. They opened up the alumni foil and placed the dope on their spoon. They put a splash of water onto the spoon as well. They grabbed their lighters, then put some heat to the metal and cooked the dope until it became liquid. Both of their eyes lit up when they looked at each other because they were about to experience a high of a lifetime. Reaching for her cotton, Nu-Nu placed it on the spoon to absorb the liquid so no air would get in to the needle and her mother did the same. The littlest air being injected into their veins could send them to an early grave. Nu-Nu then grabbed the needle off the table and stuck it into the cotton to suck up the liquid. Darlene watched her daughter. She watched her like she was amazed, but the truth of the matter was Darlene felt a little guilty for turning her daughter out. Nu-Nu then stood up, took her belt from around her waist, and tied it around her leg. With her needle in hand she counted out loud, one-two- three. That was something that she did to prepare herself as she stuck herself. As her needle attempted to meet her vein, she grew a frustrated look on her face. Her vein had clasped, and become too hard so she had to find another one. When she found that good vein, her eyes went rolling to the back of her head and once Darlene saw that, she knew it was time for her eyes to get to rolling as well.

Nu-Nu and Darlene had been getting high together for about two years, but Darlene has been high for the last twelve years. One day Nu-Nu went to visit her mom and for the first time in her life, for some apparent reason, Darlene felt comfortable with getting high in front of her daughter. Nu-Nu was intrigued with the way her mother told her how she was feeling. Darlene asked her if she wanted to try it and without any hesitation, Nu-Nu said yea. From that day forward, Nu-Nu continued to get high.

****

"I can't believe this shit. This nigga is still blowing up my phone. I hope he gives up soon because I'm tired of seeing his name flash across my screen." Jaliyah said as she tossed her phone on the lazy boy recliner that sat in the room.

"You know despite all the shit he has done to you, he really did love you."

"I'm not trying to hear that shit. That nigga never loved me. If he did, he would have never cheated on me," Jaliyah said a little frustrated. "And why are you taking up for his nigga? Fuck him."

"I'm not taking up for him, I'm just stating a fact, and just because a nigga cheat on his woman doesn't mean that he doesn't love her. I'm here with you and I love my girl dearly?"

Laughing, Jaliyah said, "You don't love her, you are in love with the thought of what could be, but you definitely don't love her. You are no different from these other niggas floating around in these streets that are playing with that four letter word and not living up to the true definition of it. Furthermore, you don't even respect her." A wide smile came across Jaliyah's face, "You placed a ring on my finger before you placed a ring on hers and I'm not even your bitch."

"I placed that ring on your finger because you were traumatized by what Apollo did to you. You a good woman and I know your worth even though he didn't."

"That shit you just let come out your mouth sounds stupid as hell," Jaliyah laughed again. "You need to be trying to know your girls worth and stop fucking with me and all those other bitches because she really is a good girl."

"What's stupid is you making it seem like your shit don't stink. We both are doing something we have no business doing. Yea, I fuck other bitches and I do know she is a good girl. Contrary to your belief, I do love my girl. Shit just happens sometimes and this is one of those times," Hodari said as he leaned in for a kiss.

Jaliyah kissed him back passionately, but she let Hodari know it wasn't going to be no fucking because Mother Nature was in town. It didn't bother him one bit because all he really wanted was his dick sucked, something that Jaliyah had mastered.

As they continued to kiss, Hodari lifted her shirt and began to play with her right nipple with his fingers. He knew how much she loved having her nipples played with; it did something to her body. He gave her nipple a nice squeeze and

Jaliyah felt her pussy getting wet, but she didn't know if it was from the blood or the moisture of her pussy. Hodari continue to tease Jaliyah, but she stopped him in his tracks. She knew she wasn't going to get any real satisfaction so she took control and pushed Hodari shoulders gently and he fell lightly onto the bed. She unzipped his pants and out popped his sausage. Her lips met his dick like a magnet. In the middle of getting his dick sucked, Jaliyah's cell phone began to ring. She didn't have to look at the caller ID to know who it was because each person that called her had their own unique ring tone.

"Hello," Jaliyah said in between of sucking Hodari's dick. All Jaliyah heard was Mariah sobbing on the other end of the phone so she immediately stopped sucking his dick. "Hello," she said again. "What wrong Mariah, talk to me."

"I thought he loved me. You told me he was going to do this to me and when I see him, I'm fucking him straight up. It's over between us. This nigga has a whole family and it's not just one bitch he's fucking, its two bitches. For all I knew, it could possibly be more," Mariah said as she continued to cry uncontrollably.

"What happened? Where are you? Do you need me to fuck Hodari up," Jaliyah said throwing question after question not giving her a chance to answer. Jaliyah really didn't give a fuck about Mariah's problems, but she knew it would make Mariah feel good that she was concerned. Jaliyah stop giving a fuck about Mariah's feelings or anyone else's feeling when love said fuck her first. She didn't care about nobody's happiness. She felt that love has never been on her side so why try to continue to concur it. Love no longer existed in her vocabulary or in her world so if she couldn't be happy the next bitch wouldn't be either.

After Jaliyah stopped with the questions, Mariah paused for a brief moment to regain her composure. She breathe heavy into the phone then she began to speak with lesser tears falling down her face even though her heart still hurt the same. "Hodari's women, girlfriends, fiancée's, whoever the bitches wanted to be e-mailed me at work today."

Mariah went into details and told her about both e-mails. Jaliyah didn't say a word. She listened as her best friend's heart let the painful incident spill from her mouth. The hold time Mariah was explaining to Jaliyah, the only thing that could be heard coming from the other end of the phone was "umm umm." Jaliyah made it seem like Mariah had her undivided attention, but the truth of the matter was she had Hodari's dick back in her mouth while he had his head back and eyes rolling enjoying the moment.

Once Mariah was finished with the story she said, "I need a drink. Can you come over? I need some company before I crack up."

Jaliyah replied with, "I'm so sorry this is happening to you, but I'm tied up at this very moment. I know your pain to well and wish I could come over right now to be with you, but give me a couple of hours and I will be there," even though she had no attention of showing up.

After ending the call with Mariah, she looked deep into Hodari eyes, gave him three nice deep throats, and sucked on the tip of his dick causing him to cum immediately. She swallowed, and then got off her knees and looked at him again, "You are in some deep shit so I don't know if it's safe for you to go home right now," she laughed.

****

Jaliyah and Hodari starting messing around a couple of weeks after Tina showed up and fucked up the wedding. Mariah told Hodari that she was worried about Jaliyah because every time she stopped by her house, there was no answer. Hodari saw the worried look on Mariah's face. He told her he knew how much Jaliyah meant her, so out the kindness of his heart, he would stop by her house to see if she would answered for him. The next day, Hodari went straight to Nu-Nu crib and let himself in with the key she had given him. Nu-Nu was out of town in Miami with a couple of her friends living life to the fullest. He knew exactly where Nu-Nu kept Jaliyah's spare key so he lifted up the bible that it rest under. He quickly snatched up the key and headed next door to Jaliyah's house. He knocked on the door several times, but there was no answer. He put his ear to the door and he heard the television on so he began to knock again, but this time he let her know it was him knocking and of course there still was no answer. He knocked a couple more times and when he realized that she wasn't going to answer the door, he let himself in with Nu-Nu's key. As soon as he entered, everything seemed normal. Her place was clean and everything seemed in place until he reached her dining room. Her dining room was as disaster. On her dining room table set her beautiful wedding gown covered in what appeared to be blood until he got close enough and noticed it was only ketchup. For a minute, he thought he was going to have to call 911 to report a homicide or a suicide. He couldn't believe how she destroyed her dress. She destroyed the dress the same way

Apollo and his bitch destroyed her heart. There were also pictures of what appeared to have been of her and Apollo, but on every picture, his head was cut off. After seeing that, Hodari knew that Apollo had really caused some internal damage to Jaliyah.

Heading toward Jaliyah's bedroom, he called out her name over the loud TV that was playing. All he could hear was Kevin Hart's voice cracking jokes as if he was lying in the bed next to her.

"Who the fuck is that in my house, I have a gun and if you come any closer, I'm going to blow your brains out," Jaliyah said with fear in her voice. While Hodari was beating on the door, Jaliyah actually didn't hear him because her TV was extremely loud and her mind was somewhere else.

"Calm down Jaliyah. It's me Hodari," he yelled out as he stopped in his tracks. He knew from seeing the mess in the dining room that Jaliyah wasn't in her right state of mind so he didn't want to become a victim over something he had nothing to do with.

"Damn Hodari, you scared me," she said while turning off the television.

"Is it safe for me to proceed," Hodari asked.

"Boy, bring your ass in here," she laughed. There was no need to ask him how he got into her house because she knew his relationship with her sister and she figured he must have used the key.

Jaliyah set up in her king size bed in her birthday suit. As soon as Hodari entered the room his eyes got big when he saw her medium sized perky brown titties and her neatly shaved pussy. He instantly felt an erecting come on. "Girl, put on some damn clothes," he spoke barely above a whisper

"This is my crib and if you don't like what you see, you can leave," Jaliyah said.

"Well, I see that my work here is done. You are not dead so I will be leaving. I was just coming over here to check on you because you had Mariah worried."

As Hodari turned to leave, Jaliyah called out his name. "Hodari, can you give this to Mariah for me and tell her I'm sorry.

Turning back around to get what Jaliyah had for Mariah, his lips where instantly met with hers and his dick fell into her right hand. Jaliyah massaged his dick until it came to a full erection. Hodari didn't resist what Jaliyah was doing to him because any man with eyes for a fine bitch wouldn't resist what was happening, even though it was with his woman's best friend and his side chick's sister. Not one time did Jaliyah stop to think that what she was doing to her best friend was wrong because she was filled with so much hurt that she couldn't think rationally. If Jaliyah was hurting from a broken heart, she wanted everybody else to hurt right along with her.

Hodari kissed her aggressively and she walked him over onto the bed. She pulled his pants down and sucked cum out of his dick. Once she finished she smiled at him and mouth the words, "Fuck love."

CHAPTER ELEVEN

Several days had passed and I hadn't heard from Hodari to get his version of the story. After I left the office that day, I went on with my day as usual. Even though the e-mails that I received broke my heart, nothing was going to steal my joy of becoming a homeowner. I met with the realtor as planned and got the keys. After that, I called Hodari's phone to confront his stupid ass, but didn't get an answer so I headed straight to his crib. I was so ready to give him a piece of my mind. Once I pulled up, I didn't see his car anywhere in sight, but I did see his mother's car so I parked my car, headed on her porch and rung her door bell. When Cookie opened the door, she greeted me with a smile and I embraced her with a hug.

"Hey momma Cookie is Hodari here," I asked already knowing the answer to my own question.

"I haven't seen Hodari in a week," she replied with a slight smirk on her face. My head dropped to my chest and my heart felt like it was about to pop out of it, but my antennas instantly went up by her response. Hodari had only spent the weekend with me the past week so I knew his trifling ass had been up to no good.

Unfaithful bastard was written all over him and I could only imagine where he's been sticking his dick. I'm sure he's been at his baby momma house or that other bitch house. These niggas these days don't appreciate a good woman until she's gone. I wanted to die instantly at the thought of Hodari being a father already. It broke my heart to know that someone else's kids are walking around with his blood flowing through their veins. Hodari bitch ass already knew he had a family; this is probably why he kept missing our appointments at the fertility clinic. He never wanted to start a family with me he was all talk. I hate Hodari. I hate I even allowed him into my heart. I should have known better to fall in love with the rebound man. If Hodari hid his hoes and kids, I wonder what else his sneaky ass could be hiding. I so badly wanted to break down in front of his mother, but I couldn't let her see me weak, that would have made her day. When I decided to go to Hodari's house, I wasn't expecting his sneak dissing ass mother to give me confirmation that her son was out in the streets cheating. All I wanted was for Hodari to be home so I could get some answers.

After lifting my head from my chest, I took a deep breath before I began to speak. I knew if I didn't, my voice was going to crack from the pain I was feeling. "Cookie, if you talk to your son before I do, can you let him know I'm looking for him. He's needs to check in with me ASAP."

Cookie shook her head up and down to indicate that she would do what I asked of her, but I knew nine times out of ten, she wouldn't relay my message. Cookie was messy like that and by the expression that was plastered on my face; she was going to do everything in her power to keep it that way. She didn't want to see me happy especially not with her son and I had a feeling that her grandkids and his fiancée might be the reason why. Cookie hated me just as much as I hated her, but we phony kicked it and tolerated each other because of Hodari. Cookie and I could have been the best of friends, but sometimes she thought Hodari was her man instead of her son and I had a big problem with that.

****

Having a slight headache, I sat on my couch and stared out the window like a zombie. I haven't had any sleep. I had just finished doing the last of my packing and on the weekend, I would be officially moving into my new place. Even though,

I was mentally drained, I can honestly say, I was happy about my new house. I just wished Hodari was here to share my happiness, which was supposed to be our happiness.

It had been exactly three days and I still hadn't heard from Hodari, and it had been weighing heavy on my heart. What did I do wrong; I questioned myself repeatedly? Why was I being punished? Was I not good enough for him or any man? As I continued to contemplate, the more I hurt and the more I needed to ease my pain. I thought about doing what I knew would take my pain away, but quickly thought twice. I was no longer going to cause myself harm on the accountability of others. My mind was all over the place and I didn't know if I wanted to forgive Hodari once I heard his side of the story so I could continue to love him or write his ass off as another nigga that had just broken my heart. Either way, I knew I would never forget.

After trying to call his phone several times with no avail while sitting on the couch, I finally decided to stop being a couch potato and take some action. If he wasn't going to answer or come to me, I was going to him because this shit needed to be set straight. I had my mind made up on what my next move was going to be. I looked at the clock on my burnt orange wall and the time was 6:42 a.m. The early bird catches the worm and I was about to catch his ass. This nigga just didn't know that he had me going crazy and I was about to do some shit out of the ordinary. Doing things that I would have never done if I was in my right state of mind, but when a man gets inside your heart, there is no telling what you would do.

It had just broke daylight when I pulled up in front of Hodari's crib and again his car was nowhere in sight. It wasn't in his mother's driveway, parked in front of the crib, or up the street. I was ready to camp out. I mean literally camp out and I wasn't moving out that spot until I had a face to face with him. I was either going to catch him coming or going and I hope he was prepared for what I had for his ass. I didn't know how long I was going to have to wait for him. I didn't know if I was going to be hours or days so before I left my house, I grabbed my cooler and filled it with ice. I made me a couple of sandwiches, grabbed a couple bottles of water, and tossed it in there. I then grabbed two big bags of chips off the refrigerator, a roll of tissue out the bathroom and a bucket. I wasn't leaving from in front of his house until I saw him and I meant that.

From Hodari's disappearing act, I was almost certain that he knew about his bitches contacting me. He was probably somewhere thinking of a lie to tell me, but at that point, all I wanted was the truth. All I wanted to know was why. Once I got my answers and depending on how he answered the questions that was going to determine if I was going to walking away.

After that thought, my mind drew a blank for a couple of seconds. It was as if I was somewhere in space then I came back to reality. Fuck that, fuck that nigga, he has a whole family that I never knew exist so I didn't even know why I was second guessing on what I was going to do about my relationship with him. I was going to leave his punk ass no matter what. I tried to pump myself up to leave him and think about all the wrong he has ever done to me, but I couldn't. I couldn't think of nothing. For all I know, those hoes were lying on my man. Hodari has never hurt me or caused harm to me so why am I taking the word of some bitches I never laid eyes on. At that very moment, I knew that no matter what Hodari said to me or no matter when he showed up, I was going to accept him back with open arms. I wasn't going to let anybody come in between of what we had and was trying to build.

As I waited patiently in the car, I decided to have a talk with God. I was raised in the church so I always had my faith despite what I'd been going through. "God, please hear me. Hear me now lord. I need you more than ever. I can't go back through the heartache that I went through before. I need you to protect my heart. My last relationship damn near destroyed me. It brought me to my knees several times and it damn near drove me to commit suicide because the pain was so unbearable. No woman should have to endure what I went through or possibly might be going through now. That relationship with Tyheem, took away everything I had in me. It took away my confidence, my dignity, and my peace of mind. I wanted to say fuck love so badly, but when Hodari found me all of that change. I don't think I would have bounced back that fast if it wasn't for him. I almost let my past determine my future because my last relationship took me through hell and back. Not only did he cheat on me; he cheated on me with a transvestite and Hodari was there to pick up the pieces so I'm not understanding why he would put this hurt on me that I couldn't bear. Lord, I beg you, please protect my heart." After having my talk, I closed my eyes and when I opened them, a tear fell freely down both cheeks.

As I continued to sit in my car, I thought about all the different levels of hurt that I've ever been through. From childhood on up to adulthood, every man that has come into my life has hurt me. What have I done to get this type of treatment? Maybe, it wasn't meant for me to be happy or to be in love. The pain…Lord, the pain that I was feeling broke me down and I wanted so badly for the pain to go away. Tears continue to escape my eyes and they were coming uncontrollably. Each time I wiped a tear away with the back of my hand, more followed. It felt like I was about to have a nervous breakdown because I couldn't control my tears. My phone began to vibrate causing me to jump. Just for a moment, a slight smile came across my face because something told me in my heart that it was Hodari calling, but when I looked at my phone I became disappointed. It was a friend request from Facebook. I went straight to Facebook and went to my friend request list and there sit the same friend request that I ignored days before, 'BoomIGotYourMan.' Whoever this bitch was, wanted to be a part of my world so bad and I know it had something to do with Hodari. I didn't know if it was Keisha, the other bitch or a new bitch. Whoever it was, I was going to give them exactly what they were looking for.

At this point, I figured I couldn't get any more hurt than what I already was. After accepting the friend request, I instantly went browsing through her pictures to get a glimpse of her life. All she had was selfies. She had no pictures with friends or family. Her page was all about her. I didn't put anymore thought into the chick or her page all I wanted was for that nigga Hodari to pop up.

CHAPTER TWELEVE

Jaliyah had just finished making up Hodari's bed and fluffy up his pillows when she heard him on the phone with Nu-Nu. She didn't even bother to ask him what she wanted because she already knew the answer. Jaliyah have had Hodari occupied for the last couple of days and he haven't had any contact with anybody besides her. They have been tucked away at his crib that no one knew about besides her. Yea, he lived in his mother's basement, but any real nigga that was in the streets had an extra crib somewhere.

"So what are you going to tell Mariah and Nu-Nu when you see them?" Jaliyah asked as she grabbed her overnight bag from the side of the bed.

"I owe Nu-Nu no explanation, she's not my bitch, but Mariah, I'll think of something to tell her. She believes anything that comes out my mouth anyway so it won't be hard to convince her," Hodari said as he slipped on his jogging pants.

"Growing up with her, I always knew she was a weak bitch for a nigga, but I don't think things are going to go as smooth as you think this time. The shit she was telling me has to have some truth to it."

"So you still not going to tell me what she told you."

"You know what, why not," Jaliyah smiled roguishly.

Jaliyah went into details about what Mariah told her. Hodari mouth just stood wide opened until she finished with the story. He didn't attempt to interrupt her one bit, but when she finished, all he could do was shake his head.

"That bitch," he yelled. "Something told me to just drop the money off then leave. I knew once I gave her this dick she was going to start acting a fool." Jaliyah eyes got bucked and Hodari had her undivided attention. "There is some truth to that story?" Hodari said. "Am I engaged, no…Have I ever been engaged, yes…Do I have kids…no, well…something like that, I mean yes, but they are not biologically mine. Keisha and I were childhood sweethearts. I thought we were going to be together forever, but when the judicial system separated us my world fell apart. I went to jail for two years for trafficking weed back and forth from Chicago to Wisconsin. Since this was my first offense, they gave me the two years calling it a light sentence. While in jail, Keisha cheated on me and got pregnant back to back by my rivalry and that broke me in two. When I got out, she begged me for my forgiveness and I accepted her back into my life with open arms after my eyes landed on her kids. I was a sucker when it came to kids. Two weeks after Keisha and I got back together, a stray bullet killed the father of her kids. I then asked Keisha for her hand in marriage and told her I would protect her, love her, and I wanted to place my name on the kid's birth certificate. Keisha wouldn't have wanted things any other way. The next day we went to the Cook County Clerk's office, got our marriage license and I signed my name on the kid's birth certificate gracefully. I didn't want Keisha kids to grow up the way that I did. I wanted to give her kids a happy home, a stable home with a mother and father. If I was going to be a permanent part of Keisha life, it was only right that I do right by her kids, but our relationship didn't last long. Keisha couldn't keep her legs closed long enough to become Mrs. Edward. My money wasn't coming in fast enough for her so she did exactly what a hoe would do. Fuck for some extra cash. I got a call that she was tricking off with one of the local neighborhood dope boys. My homie who had just saw her while he was going into his room called me quickly and I rush over to the hotel where she was. I kicked in the door and caught her butt naked riding his dick. I ended that relationship right then and there."

"Damn Hodari that shit is deep," Jaliyah said.

"Yea, I know. I'm still a part of her kid's life and I kept this part of my life a secret from Mariah.

He never told Mariah about Keisha and her kids because he honestly didn't believe that him and Mariah relationship was going to last. She was a wreck when they got together. Now they are three years into their relationship and he knows when he see Mariah he has a lot of explaining to do.

After Hodari finished explaining himself to Jaliyah about his past life, he turned on his phone and immediately, his phone starts vibrating for about two minutes from the text messages and the voicemail alerts that was coming through. Hodari knew without a doubt that Mariah had been trying to get through to him. He thought about calling her at the moment, but then he decided that it was best that he dealt with Mariah face to face so he decided to read some of her messages that she sent him to get an idea of her mind set. He looked through his text messages as Jaliyah stared on and to his surprise, not one of the text messages was from Mariah, they were all from Nu-Nu.

"Daddy where are you," the first text message read. "I love you," the second one read. "This pussy need you," the third message read, but after that. Nu-Nu's messages turned hateful. "Nigga, I know your bitch ass see me calling and texting you....I'm fucking you up when I see you...I hope you die....I hope your momma die. I hope that bitch you fucking burn you....Nigga I hope you catch AIDS." Her very last message read, "Why are you doing this to me."

Hodari shook his head and hated that he let pussy control him at times. Pussy was his weakness especially good pussy, but he knew he had to hurry and get his shit together before all his skeletons came busting out the closet.

CHAPTER THIRTEEN

"Hey baby," I heard Hodari say.

I jumped at the sound of his voice. I was watching the movers load my last box on the back of the moving truck. How dare he show up after all these days as if nothing has happened? I quickly turned around and smacked him without saying a word.

"Ouch…what the fuck you do that for?" he asked while throwing the dozen of roses he had for me on the ground.

The only time this nigga come baring gifts is when he's guilty of something and the verdict was already in.

Nigga, don't play stupid, you know why. Ask the hoe you been with these last couple of days, your baby momma, your fiancée. Oops…Your two fiancée's. Which one were you with…huh."

Hodari just stood there with a dumb ass look on his face, before he spoke. "Baby let me explain.

"There is nothing to explain. You fucked up and it's over between us. I'm done seriously," I said playing hardball.

When those words escaped my mouth, I knew I didn't mean them. I just wanted him to feel hurt because I was hurting. I really wanted to run into his arms because I missed him so much, but the truth of the matter was he fucked up and I wasn't going to let him off that easy. He definitely had some explaining to do.

"Baby, don't say that. I love you. Things are not what they seem," Hodari said sincerely.

"Things are what they seem so fuck you and your fraudulent ass ways." I was pissed and I meant every word I said at that very moment.

I looked at Hodari for a brief moment with disgust. I wanted to spit in his fucking face. It took everything I had in me not to spit on his sorry ass so I rushed into the empty house before I did something that I would regret. Walking swiftly, I felt his presence behind me. I searched for my purse that I had the e-mails in hoping I didn't mistakenly pack it away. When I spotted my purse, I powered walked to it, with Hodari still on my heels. I reached in my purse, pulled out the papers, and smacked him dead in the face with them.

"What's this," he asked as he reached for the papers.

"Read it, you dumb motherfucker," I said pissed. I think I was more pissed at myself than him because I knew I couldn't walk away from the relationship. He had a hold on my heart like no other.

Hodari eyes glanced over the papers and a smile crept upon his face. I wanted to smack the shit out of him again, but I waited to see what the smile was all about.

"This is some bullshit," he said. "Baby, take a seat." I looked around at him like he was a fool. Where in the hell was I going to sit? The house was empty. There wasn't a chair, a stool, or couch in sight. He saw the expression on my face, took me by my hand, and led me to the floor. "I'm sorry about all of this. This is the type of shit she does."

"Who is she," I asked trying to figure out which hoe he was speaking in reference to.

"Keisha, the bitch is crazy and this is not her first time doing this."

"Doing what, you better start explaining quickly," I said impatiently.

Hodari went into detail about his prior life with Keisha. He also mentioned there was no other fiancée. He told me that Keisha sent both e-mail trying to make the situation worse than what is was. He also went into detail about the kids. I'm not going to lie; I was a little envious of the kids because I wanted my kids to be the first to call him daddy, but I respected him even more as a man for stepping up and taking on that responsibility. He asked me to accept his apology for not telling him about the kids and I accepted without thinking twice.

"I'm sorry for over-reacting," I said as I reached and grabbed his face bringing it closer to mine for a kiss. We kissed for about two minutes before our lips parted. I loved Hodari; I'm not going to lie. He meant the world to me and I was going to do whatever it took to make our relationship work.

Hodari and I chatted for a while longer. We went into detail about the house and he said that next weekend he would have all of his stuff packed and ready to move into our new place together. I was excited so excited that I didn't even care any longer how Keisha stumbled upon my e-mail, the mysterious Facebook friend request, or the fact that I haven't seen him nor spoken with him. All I care about was having my man in my presence at that very moment.

****

"We have to stop this," I said to my ex-boyfriend Traye while he was on his knees giving me the best head ever.

122

Traye didn't have any reaction to what I had just said as he held my legs up in the air. He just kept licking all around my pussy walls trying to make me cum. I tried to push his head from between my legs, but he wasn't having it. His neck game was too strong for me so I just sat back and enjoyed what he was giving me.

The whole time he was eating my pussy, I couldn't take my mind off Hodari. I started to feel guilty for what I was doing especially since I got confirmation that he wasn't being unfaithful to me. Hodari would definitely kill me if he knew I was lying on a blow up mattress at my old crib enjoying the pleasures of another man. Hodari knew all about me and Traye's past relationship. He have told me to end our friendship plenty of times because he didn't believe people that have fucked couldn't be friends, but I ignored his request. I tried my best to convince him that we haven't had sex in years, since we had been a couple and that actually was the truth, but he wasn't trying to hear nothing that came out my mouth. Hodari didn't want any man around me, but him. Traye actually was the close friend that let me rent out the house that I was living in before I bought my house. His mother died and left him the house and he couldn't see himself living in it or selling it so he rented it out to make some extra cash.

After making me cum, Traye came up for air and finally responded. "Stop what, I'm just getting started." Traye then fell on top of me lightly and pulled my shirt up exposing my bra. He popped my titties out and engulfed the left one sucking it gently. I moan in pleasure a couple of times before I yelled out stop again.

Tray stopped because he heard the seriousness in my voice. "Listen Traye, I'm serious. We have to stop fucking around. Hodari and I are back together."

"I knew your dumb ass wasn't going to stay away from that nigga. No matter what he does to you, you will always go back."

"Traye, who the fuck you calling dumb," I said raising my voice.

"Calm down Mariah, there's no need to get loud, but the truth hurts doesn't it. I'm your best friend and your lover, I know you like the back of my hands."

"Correction…You are my best friend and just because we fucked a couple of times within a week don't make us lovers so check that shit."

"I don't know any other way to say it Mariah, but I know I told you my feelings for you were gone, but girl, I truly love you and always will. I don't want to see you hurting. You just need to leave him and let me take care of you. We will be happy together." Traye said while gazing into my eyes.

I was shocked by Traye's confession to me. I loved him, but I wasn't in love with him. Our time as a couple has come and gone so my heart didn't beat the same way for him like it used to. We were friends, best friends at that and Traye needed to get his feelings back in check. My heart only beat for one person and that was Hodari.

"Traye, you need to put those feelings you have for me in a big black box and throw that motherfucker far away. I refuse to go back down that road with you. Now, I hate I even let you in my personal business because I know you've been praying on the downfall of my relationship." After receiving those e-mails that day at work, I didn't know where or who to turn to. I called the source of the problem and I didn't get a response from him. I called Jaliyah and she acted like she was too damn busy for me so I called the only other person who I knew would be there for me and that was Traye.

Back in the day Traye and I had a unique relationship. It was different from any other relationship that I have had. He opened and closed doors for me, sent flowers to my job and we had date night once a week. He was a gentleman to say the least. Even though we loved each other, we knew our relationship would never work despite how hard we tried or how we felt about each other. Our two year relationship ended because we came from two different worlds. He was a Muslim and I was a Christian. His Muslim beliefs were too strong for me and there was no way in the world I was going to allow him to have several wives. Over the course of the years, our love attraction blossomed into a friendship that could never be broken.

I got up off the mattress and got myself together. I saw the pissed look in his eyes, but I didn't care. "Traye, I have no business being here. I must go."

"Let's talk about this," he said as he pulled at my arm, but I jerk away from him.

I didn't respond to him. I hate I had to do this to Traye because he was a good friend, but I had to stay far away from him as possible. We had no reason to see or call each other especially since I no longer rented the house from him.

As I gathered my purse and car keys off the floor, I heard someone banging on the door. It sounded like someone was upset about something the way the knocks were coming. My heart dropped to the pit of my stomach because I thought about Hodari being on the other side of the door. Something told me to park my car inside of the garage, but I didn't think anybody would be coming here looking for me since I moved. I looked at Traye's perfect, yet upset face. His hair was wild like a mop, but it went perfect with his bushy eyebrows. His pencil lips finally part and asked, "Who the fuck is that knocking at the door. Are you expecting somebody?"

CHAPTER FOURTEEN

Pulling up in front of Hodari's house, Nu-Nu was pissed because she hasn't been able to get in contact with him.

She didn't have a clue as to why Hodari was giving her the cold shoulder when in actuality; she should have been the one giving him the cold shoulder. He was the one that lied about coming back to her house, she haven't heard from him in days and on top of that, he was trying to start a family with Mariah and that was something that didn't sit well with her at all. In Nu-Nu's mind, if she couldn't have his baby no other bitch would be walking around producing his seed. After having that talk with her mother, Nu-Nu found the courage that she had been looking for and she was no longer questioning herself. She knew exactly what she had to do to have her man all to herself so death became the only thing on her mind every time she thought about Mariah, but she was going to torture her first before she had the pleasure of ending her life.

After riding to Hodari's crib looking for him and getting upset that he wasn't there, Nu-Nu figured she would head to her next stop. She believed that if Hodari wasn't at her crib or his own crib, he had to be at Mariah's.

Pulling away from the curb Nu-Nu headed in the direction of what she believed to be Mariah's house. She had no clue that Mariah had moved. Once Nu-Nu pulled up to Mariah's old neighborhood, she glanced around the suburban area and searched for Hodari's car. Upset, she hit her steering wheel when she notice his car wasn't anywhere in sight. *Where the fuck is this nigga,* she thought. She tried hitting his line, but didn't get an answer. She had been hitting his line for the last couple of days with the same results.

Before Nu-Nu went to her mom's house the other day, she had planned to pop up at Mariah's house to let her know that her man had been up to no good, and since Hodari wasn't around now, now would be a good time to enlighten her on his infidelities. If Hodari didn't want to leave Mariah, she was going to give Mariah a reason to leave him.

Nu-Nu reached on the side of the door, grabbed her mace, and placed it in her purse. She did that in case Mariah wanted to get out of hand when she delivered the news of how unfaithful her man has been. Nu-Nu then got out her car and looked around again to double check to see if she saw Hodari's car and she didn't. What she did notice was how nice the suburban neighborhood was compared to where she was from. There was no court way buildings insight, only big beautiful houses with manicured lawns. Mariah's house was tucked away from the city lights and rowdy-thugs, which was something she was accustomed to as a child, but once she got older, she found a new way of life.

Nu-Nu turned her nose up after glancing at Mariah's house and her nice foreign car that set in the driveway. Then she prepared for the walk of doom that was going to break Mariah's heart. As Nu-Nu walked toward the front door, she rehearsed in her head what she was going to say. She tried to think of a nice way to say, 'I'm fucking your man, and he loves me so back the fuck off,' but there was no nice way to say it. No matter how she said it, Mariah heart was going to break in two.

Nu-Nu banged on the door with an attitude. She banged on the door like somebody was after her, like someone was literally trying to kill her. "Damn, who is it?" Mariah screamed from the other side of the door. Nu-Nu didn't say a word, but an evil smile did come across her face. All she could do was think about the hurt she was going to cause Mariah and the victory she was going to receive. Nu-Nu heard Mariah getting closer as her heels click clacked on the wood floor so she started back beating on the door. "Who the fuck is it?" Mariah yelled out again, but this time Nu-Nu responded.

"Just open the door."

The door swung opened and Nu-Nu stared Mariah dead in her eyes. "What's up Nu-Nu is everything alright," Mariah said as she stood at the door with her hands on her hip.

Nu-Nu noticed the small cuts around Mariah wrist, but didn't elaborate on it. "Umm, Umm…"

"What the fuck, cat got your tongue? You were just beating on the door like a mad woman and now you ain't got shit to say. What the fuck do you want Nu-Nu? Why are you here?"

"Girl, calm your square ass down. I was in the neighborhood and my cousin told me to stop by to check on you. She said she has been trying to get in contact with you and you haven't been answering your phone."

Mariah began to laugh. She then looked down at her phone that was in her hand then back up at Nu-Nu. "You scared me there for a minute. I didn't know what to think, but I will call your cousin first chance I get. I haven't received any calls from her though, but if you talk to her before I do just tell her I'm good."

"Ok, cool." Nu-Nu said before she walked away.

Nu-Nu headed back to her car then pulled off immediately. She drove for about two minutes before she found a park around the corner and turned off her engine. She sat in silence for a minute, trying to figure out why she froze up when she saw Mariah, she was far from scary; she was straight hood. She was more than pissed with herself for not following through with her plan. It only took her a moment before she flipped the script. She began to hit her steering wheel several times and with every hit, a curse word followed. "Bitch...Motherfucker....fuck...fuck....fuck...."

Nu-Nu began to cry and her eyes turned blood shot red. Through her tears, she picked up her phone to call Hodari again. She pressed each number as fast as she could and by the time she put the phone up to her ear, she heard Hodari's voice. "I'm busy Nu-Nu so make it quick."

"Fuck you and fuck love," she said then hung up the phone.

Nu-Nu continued to sob. She then spoke out loud to herself again. "No motherfucker is about to play with my heart. When I wanted to leave his ass, he should have let me go. Now there is no leaving me. He is stuck with me for the rest of his life."

After Nu-Nu finished talking to herself, she started her car back up and circled the block only to end up back in front of Mariah's house. By this time, there was an older white couple on the porch holding hands, rocking back and forth on their vintage porch swing. She smiled at them because they had exactly what she wanted, pure love. She sat in front of Mariah's house and debated if she wanted to knock on her door again, but instead she came up with another plan. One way or another she was going to figure out her man wasn't faithful even if she had to let her know indirectly.

After waiting patiently, Mr. and Mrs. Happy Couple finally went into the house after about thirty minutes. Nu-Nu kept her car running and before exiting the car, she checked her surroundings to make sure nobody else was outside enjoying the beautiful weather. The coast was clear. She lifted her armrest, grabbed her switchblade, and exited the car, leaving the driver's door open. She then ran up on Mariah's black S550, sliced all four tires, then ran back to her car passing the driver's door only to end up at her trunk. She popped the trunk as she continued to watch her surroundings. She searched her junky trunk for her white spray paint can she used to spray paint her wood chair for her bedroom. Before slamming her trunk, she looked over to make sure Mariah wasn't looking out the window and of course she wasn't. Next, she slammed her trunk down and ran back over to Mariah's car and spray painted *our man* in bold letters on the driver side door.

Nu-Nu hurried back to her car, pulled off, and headed straight to her crib. She drove like a bat out of hell riding through those suburban streets praying the police didn't pull her over. She jumped on I-290 and headed back to the west side. She was back out west in less than twenty-five minutes. When she pulled up, she saw Jaliyah getting out of Hodari's car.

CHAPTER FIFTEEN

Apollo woke up at 11:00 a.m. with Tina trying to jump on his dick. He was still drunk and halfway sleep after the wild long night they had together so having sex was the last thing on his mind. He rolled over on his side only to be rolled back over by Tina. He sighs in exhaustion after he felt her jerking on his dick. His dick rose to attention, but he didn't have the energy to put it on her.

He pushed Tina's hand away from his dick. "Not right now, Apollo mumbled.

"Come on bae, give me some dick," Tina said sexually while trying to grab back at his manhood.

He pushed her hand away again. "Seriously, not right now Tina. I'm tired. I'm drained and didn't I just fuck the shit out of you last night."

Tina smacked her lips. "I remember when there were times you fucked me every single night. You've changed ever since Jaliyah has been out of the picture."

Apollo didn't reply. He closed his eyes and threw the cover over his head. Tina pulled the cover from over his head without any hesitation.

"Girl, gone with that bullshit, I'm not up for it right now. Just let me get some rest," screamed Apollo agitated.

Tina took her hand and shoved it at his head causing his head to jerk back. Apollo didn't like that one bit. He didn't even think twice about what he was about to do. He raised his hand and smacked her across her face so hard that her brown face turned red. He then bald his fist up, and punched her in the face. Tina instantly curled up in a fetal position while covering her face.

"Bitch, look at me. Look at me now," he screamed. Tina was reluctant to do what was asked of her, but she knew she had to obey his orders. As soon as she looked up, he struck her again in the face.

"Apollo, stop. I'm sorry," she screamed out in fear.

"There's no need to be sorry. All you had to do was leave me the fuck alone when I asked you to, but naw, you had to keep fucking with me," he said then smacked her again.

Apollo then wraps his right hand around her 26-inch, two-toned weave and dragged her off his king sized round bed. She fell to the floor and bumped her head. She was dazed, but only for a minute. He then bald his fist back up and punched her some more. She yelled out in agonizing pain, but he didn't let that stop him from stomping her a couple more times. She bald back up into a ball, but that didn't stop him from throwing his punches. He punched her so much that her body became numb so she didn't feel the pain anymore. Apollo had begun to despise Tina and if looks could kill, she would have been dead a long time ago. He hated that he let the real love of his life get away, and he misses her more and more as each day pass.

Apollo walked away from Tina and left her on the floor sobbing. He walked over to the bedroom window and raised it as far as it could go. "Bitches are going to learn to listen to me," he blurted out. He walked back over toward Tina and dragged her by her arms. She began kicking and screaming to the top of her lungs. Tina felt that her life was about to end the closer they got to the window.

"No Apollo, nooo. I love you," she cried out repeatedly, but Apollo wasn't paying her any attention. Her words vanished into the air. Everything she said fell on deaf ears.

If Tina would have left Apollo alone when he was trying to get some rest, he wouldn't be all over her ass so in his eyes, Tina bought this on herself. Tina continued to cry out in pain. She prayed that the beating would be all over with soon, but Apollo had other plans for her. He didn't let up on the slaps. He slapped her several more times taking all of his built up anger out on her. Apollo wasn't just upset because of Tina not allowing him to sleep; he was upset because Tina fucked up his life. Jaliyah has been ignoring every attempt he made to contact her. The only time he was able to hear Jaliyah's voice was when her voicemail popped on.

Every time Apollo thought about Jaliyah, he blamed Tina for his problems even though he was in charge of his own actions. In his eyes, all Tina had to do was play the position that was given to her from the very beginning, instead of showing up at the wedding to ruining his life.

Finally making it to the window, he brought Tina to her feet. "Jump," he said as Tina looked at him with pleading eyes. "Bitch I said jump." She didn't bulge. Apollo lived on the seventh floor in a mini high rise building up North and anybody in their right state of mind would not have obeyed his demand. Tina knew if she jumped, death was going to be her only outcome. "Kill yourself, before I kill your stupid ass," he barked.

Apollo noticed that Tina wasn't about to commit suicide so he punched her in her stomach causing her to bend over and drugged her over to the living room balcony. She kicked and screamed every step of the way. She even bit his hand thinking that was going to help with getting her turned loose, but all that did was anger him more and he punched her in the eye. Tina never saw Apollo act like this before. Yes, he has smacked her around a time or two, threw some verbal threats out, and verbally abused her, but nothing has ever been to this point. Once they got over to the balcony, he hung her over it by her feet. Tina blood rushed to her head immediately as her heart jumped out her chest as she continued to scream. Apollo didn't care that it was mid-morning. He didn't care if the people in the building heard him. At that point he didn't care about nothing, he just let his anger consume him.

While her body dangled over the balcony, he chanted, "Next time listen and it will never get to this point." He then pulled her up and she fell into his arms crying hysterically. He pushed her away from him, than spat on her and walked away.

Apollo knew that what he had just done to Tina was to the extreme, but he had to take his built up anger out on somebody. The love that he once displayed for Tina was slowly fading away. All he wanted was Jaliyah back in his life and he was going to do whatever it took to get her back, even if it meant leaving Tina alone completely. Apollo knew that if he left Tina, there was a good chance that he could get Jaliyah back in his life.

The rest that Apollo had planned on getting was out of the question. He headed to his room and threw on something comfortable. He searched his closet until he came across a pair of Adidas jogging pants with the matching shirt. He laughed because he knew how much Jaliyah hated him to wear jogging pants. It showed off his dick print. He would always tell her that she was the only crotch watcher in the world because nobody paid attention to his dick, but her.

Once Apollo was dressed, he left the house without saying a word to Tina. He wanted to apologize for his actions because he felt kind of bad, but he decided against it. Tina was going to learn to respect the words that came out his mouth and if she didn't she was going to get her ass beat every time she didn't listen.

****

What the fuck is this nigga car doing parked in front of Jaliyah's crib, Apollo thought. Then he remembered that Hodari was fucking on Nu-Nu. Apollo sat in his car and smoked a Newport short, while searching for the right words to say to Jaliyah to win her heart back. He cracked his window as he continued to stare across the streets into Hodari's car. He thought about calling him because they haven't hung out lately, but he was on mission. Now wasn't the time. He could talk to Hodari another time. Apollo took three pulls of his cigarette and scrunched his eyes as he focused in on the passenger that was in Hodari's car. He thought his mind was playing tricks on him, but he couldn't second guess himself because the proof was right in front of his face. The female that sat in the car was a shade darker than Nu-Nu, but the exact shade as Jaliyah. Apollo was wondering why was Jaliyah sitting in the passenger side of Hodari car, but his curiosity didn't last long when he saw Hodari and Jaliyah kiss before she existed the car.

Jaliyah got out the car with a huge smile on her face. She then threw her black overnight bag on her shoulder and switched her phat ass into her apartment building never paying any attention to her surroundings. If she would have, she would have saw Apollo parked across the street, but then

141

again probably not. He was parked a couple of feet away from her building behind Hodari, but on the opposite side of the street.

Apollo popped his lock to his door heated. Steam was seeping from his pores. He was getting ready to go kick Hodari ass and then go upstairs to Jaliyah house to beat her ass. He felt disrespected. In Apollo's sick head he and Jaliyah were still together, they were a couple and she had no business locking lips with his friend. Apollo felt deep in his heart that Hodari was digging his girl from the first time he bought her around, but he never thought he would react on it. Little did Apollo know, it wasn't Hodari doing, it was Jaliyah who approached Hodari. If Jaliyah would have never stuck her tongue down his throat and grabbed his dick, Hodari would have never landed in her bed.

Apollo opened the driver door and simultaneously the passenger door open. Nu-Nu jumped in and spoke quickly, "Yea, I seen that shit too."

CHAPTER SIXTEEN

Leaving out of my old crib, my heart dropped instantly. I ran up to my car and noticed the damaged that was done to it. The four flat tires and the humiliating words that were neatly wrote on it sent me into a rage. I ran back into the house and called out Traye's name.

"What's up, he answered me nonchalantly.

"Hodari's baby momma just fucked my car up," I yelled causing my words to echo through the empty house.

"And what are you telling me for, that's your problem not mine. Remember you just told me you were through with me. Call your man, I'm sure he will come and help you. As a matter of fact, give me my key and get out because you are no longer a tenant," Traye said with a straight face meaning every word of it.

I was pissed by his response, but I couldn't be mad with Traye because he was right. I went in my purse, grabbed his key, and threw it at him, hitting him in the face. I then turned around and walked out his crib with my eyes watering up.

As I stood outside in the summer heat feeling embarrassed, a tear finally escaped my eyes and rolled down my cheeks. I felt embarrassed because I had just shitted on Traye because I was back happy with Hodari and now that I need him, Traye turned his back on me and kicked me out his house. The one person that I could always turn to in my time of need has become my enemy. At this point, I was so over Traye, I had other things to worry about. I leaned against my car thinking about who had the audacity to come to what used to be my comfort zone and fuck up my personal property. I didn't know much about Keisha, but from my brief conversation with Hodari about her, this seems like something she would do so when I saw her I was going to beat her ass with no questions asked. Hodari was going to show me where she lived and if he didn't, I was going to beat his ass. Seconds later, I scratched my head the wheels in my head didn't stop turning. I thought about the bitch on Facebook who kept sending me a friend request. I didn't know much about her, but if she was fucking with Hodari, she was a ratchet bitch. He love ratchet bitches so she was definitely a suspect. I started to hate Hodari all over again because the things that were happening to me have been because of him. I wanted to scream to the top of my lungs, but before I got a chance to, my mind wondered to my uninvited guest Nu-Nu. She had just left the premises, but why would she fuck up my car. I thought long and hard to see if we ever had an altercation and we hadn't, but I was almost certain she did this to my car because if my car was damaged when she knocked on the door, I'm sure she would have said something. I was at a loss for words. I couldn't believe that shit. Hodari sure knows how to pick them. My hand rested on the back of my neck and I massaged it. I then tilted my head back and rolled my eyes in the back of my head so my tears wouldn't fall, but I couldn't stop them, they fell anyway. I didn't want to believe that Nu-Nu was fucking my man, but from the looks of things she was.

I had so much going on inside my head that I couldn't think straight, but before I jumped to any conclusion, I was going to go and talk to Nu-Nu like a woman. I was going to ask her if she was fucking my man without sugar coating it. If she was bold enough to damage my car, I know she would be bold enough to admit she had been sleeping with my man. I didn't want to call Hodari at this point. He would have flipped out on me if he pulled up and saw Traye's car in the driveway and that was one argument I was trying to avoid so

I decided to call Jaliyah and told her what happened and she rushed to me side.

****

"Jaliyah," I called out her name to get her attention.

"What's up," she responded as she sipped on her glass of wine. She walked around my house for the first time admiring it. She smiled as she entered and exit each room. In the short amount of time, I've been living at my new place I had got a lot done. My house was damn near furnished with the exception of three out of the five bedrooms.

"Why didn't you tell me your sister was fucking my man," I asked catching her off guard. She almost choked on her wine.

"What are you talking about Mariah? How do you know Nu-Nu is sleeping with Hodari," she replied.

I wasn't sure if she was making a statement or asking a question, but I proceeded, "Because she was the one that fucked up my car. Well, I think she fucked up my car.

"I thought you said that crazy bitch fucked up your car that Hodari co-parent with."

I told Jaliyah everything Hodari told me about Keisha and her kids. I also told her, I believed she was the one that messed up my car, I

146

never mentioned Nu-Nu's name. When Jaliyah came and picked me up the other day. I didn't want to tell her off bat that I think her sister was sleeping with my man. I wanted to get proof first, but I couldn't find any so there I was a week later picking at her brain.

When Jaliyah met me at my old crib to help me with my car, we waited on the tow truck and told him where I wanted him to take my car. I told him to tow it to the city to one of Hodari's friend tire shop. Once there, we waited patiently for the tires to get fix. After my tires were fixed, I jumped in my car feeling embarrassed as I drove through the streets to an auto body shop with Jaliyah not too far behind. I got a good estimation on the paint job so I left my car their then we headed to Midway airport to get me a rental car. After I got my rental car, we went our separate ways because she had something to do. Now here we are three days later and I'm picking her head to see if she can help with my suspicion.

I went into details about why I thought Nu-Nu was the one that messed up my car and she didn't show any reaction, she just listened attentively. Once I finished, all she could muster up to say was, "Wow." There was a quick awkward moment between us, but then she spoke.

"I don't think Nu-Nu and Hodari is messing around. You need to focus on that baby momma of his."

"You right and I will," I said lying through my teeth.

Jaliyah and I laughed and talked about the good old days and the trouble we used to get up into when we were kids. She stayed about two more hours with me before Hodari walked in. They spoke and chatted for a minute then Jaliyah left going her separate way.

"Hey babe, I miss you." Hodari spoke as he leaned in for a kiss.

Without speaking back, I kissed him back giving him some tongue action.

"So when do your car get out the shop," he asked.

"It should be ready this weekend," I replied.

"Okay cool. I'm going to drop some money into your account so you can pay for it."

"Thank you baby," I said with a smiled plastered upon my face.

"Anything for the one and only lady in my life," he said lying through his fucking teeth. "Did you get a change to ask anybody at the beauty shop if they saw who hit your car," Hodari asked.

"Bae, if they did see something, there isn't anything that I can do about it now. I'm sure the driver didn't have any insurance that's why they kept going so it will be a waste of my time to hunt the person down."

I lied to Hodari about why my car was in the shop. I wanted to approach this situation the right way. I could have easily went off on him, but that wouldn't have gotten anything solve. Believe me, when the time is right, he will be approached about the situation, but until then, I was going to look for the bitch that fucked up my car.

After our brief conversation about my car, we headed in our room and made love. Hodari fell asleep immediately afterward. I called his name to make sure he was sleep. I even went as far as to shake him to try to wake him up and he didn't bulge. That was my cue to go in his pocket to get his phone so I could go throw it.

Once I grabbed his phone, I went in our master bathroom and closed the door behind me. I literally asked myself out loud. "Should I really be doing this and I answered myself with, "Hell yea because I needed answers."

Quietly, I dropped the lid on the toilet and sat on it with my bare ass. I took a deep breath before I searched through Hodari's phone because

I didn't know what I was about to find. I didn't know what to expect. I was praying that I didn't find anything, but with that huge secret about Keisha and her kids, I didn't put anything past his ass anymore. I searched through his call log and I didn't see anything suspicious. All I saw were male names, not one single female name, that along was suspicious right there. I started to think that Hodari was a dick in the bootie ass nigga, but quickly erased it from my mind because my heart wouldn't survive another episode like I did with Tyheem. I then checked his voicemail and text messages and he had none. His phone was too perfect to be true. Once upon a time, I thought Hodari could do no wrong, but after the last incidents, I really didn't know the man that I was in love with like I thought I did.

Exiting the bathroom feeling somewhat of a relief, I placed his phone right back where I found it and jumped in the bed with my man as if nothing ever happened. Lying next to the man that I love was a dream come true. We finally had our own house and it felt so good so I cuddled up next to him and drifted of into a comfortable sleep.

I was in a light slumber for about twenty minutes when I heard a vibration coming from a phone on the floor. I didn't know if it was my phone or Hodari's because both of our pants were on the same side of the bed, with our phones in the pocket. I quickly looked at Hodari to make sure he was still sleep and he was. He was a hard sleeper and it takes a lot to wake him especially after good lovemaking.

I instantly grabbed Hodari's phone because my phone never rings at that time of the morning. I scooped his phone up and felt disappointed and relieved at the same time. Disappointed because there wasn't a female on the other end of the phone to catch him up and relived that it wasn't a female on his phone so I wouldn't have to deal with a broken heart.

I then turned to my phone. I wondered who in the hell was calling me at 3:00 in the morning. I was scared. I didn't know what to expect. The only thing that was going through my mind was bad thoughts. I didn't know if something had happened to my mom or someone else in my family. Whatever the case was, getting an unexpected call at 3:00 a.m. couldn't be good. I grabbed my phone from my jean pocket that rested on the floor. I looked through my call log and I didn't have a miss call. That was strange because I know that I had just heard a phone vibrating. I took it as if I was dreaming so I placed my phone back into my pocket. As soon as I got comfortable next to my man, I heard the vibrating noise again. I jumped up and grabbed my phone quickly. I noticed that I had a call coming through from Facebook, which has never happened before, but when I noticed who it was, I quietly got my naked ass out the bed and rushed into the next room.

"Hello," I said politely into my phone even though I wanted to yell out, "Bitch state your business."

"Hey girl," this chick said as if she was one of my best friends. "I'm not sure if u know of me or not, but I'm not calling you on no disrespectful shit. I'm just trying to figure out what's the real relationship between you and Hodari." I took my phone from my ear and looked at it because I felt like my ear was deceiving me, but I let the hoe continue without interrupting her. "Because from what he has told me, you and him used to mess around, y'all used to be a couple, but there are some things that's not adding up that's why I'm hitting you up. When I go through his phone, I see your number in his recent call log with lengthy conversations or recent pictures of you two so I'm coming to you to get some questions answered. Before you tell me your side of the story, let me just clear some things up. Hodari and I are not in a committed relationship, however we do fuck with each other tough, and if you guys are still in a relationship, I don't want anything to do with him because I'm not that type of woman."

I laughed briefly to myself. This bitch had some nerves. She definitely didn't call me to be friendly or to look out for me. She called for a purpose and that was to rub in my face she had been fucking my man. I thought about just simply cursing her out and hanging up on her, but I said what the hell, let me shed some light on a situation that she already knew too well.

"No, I don't know you, why should I know you, but I am glad that you reached out to me. I hope you didn't believe anything he had to say because we are indeed a couple. Not only are we a couple we have a house together and we soon will be starting a family…"

She waited no time, with stopping me from going on to my next sentence. "So are you telling me you are pregnant?"

"What I'm telling you is exactly what I said so you can take that however you want to take it," I said pacing the floor heated. I knew I hit a nerve just like she knew she hit a nerve when she called me because she became completely silent. I didn't even hear her breathing. "Are you still there," I asked.

"Yes, I'm here," she answered then there was another moment of silence, then she spoke again. "Well, you confirmed what I needed to know so you don't have to worry about me messing with your man any longer. I wish you two the best," she said then hung up the phone.

I felt like I couldn't catch a break with this nigga and these hoes. Why was everything coming to the light so rapidly? I guess God was letting me know that this nigga was no good for me. God was trying to push me away from him and actually it was starting to work.

As I was getting ready to storm in my room to confront Hodari about the call I had just received, my phone vibrated again. I was reluctant to look at my phone because I knew it was more trouble, but I looked anyway. An icon popped up on my phone to let me know I had an inbox from Facebook. I took a deep breath, then I headed backed to Facebook. As soon as I opened my inbox, I was smacked in the face. The chick had sent me a picture with a hashtag that read #TheThingsOurManDo.

When I looked at the picture, it shattered my poor heart and bought me to my knees literally. It felt like somebody knocked me off my feet and I was about to have a heart attack. I could believe my eyes. The picture was of her, Hodari, her three kids all smiled up like one big happy family, and it looked like the picture was taken at Chucky Cheese. I knew he was a sucker for kids, but damn. I shook my head repeatedly. This nigga had been playing daddy daycare with another woman's kids. What I found suspicious was the fact she had her face cover up with an emoji, the one with the tongue sticking out. This chick went out her way to call me, but at the same time, she hides her true identity. I then went to her profile picture. That's when I realized this was a phony Facebook page. Even though I couldn't see her face a blind man could see the body types were totally different.

There were no words to explain what I was feeling. I found enough energy to get off the floor. I stormed out of the room and ran downstairs to the kitchen. This nigga wasn't about to get a pass this time. I opened one of my junk drawers and grabbed the crazy glue. Next, I looked at the knives that sat on the counter and studied each one of them for a second. I was trying to figure out which one I wanted to use on Hodari. I didn't know if I wanted to inflict him with small wounds or large ones. I shook my head at my damn self. I felt like a fool standing there studying them knives as if they were an exam. I quickly snatched the closest one to me and then I headed toward the stairs that led up to my bedroom. All type of horrific thoughts was going through my head. Hodari promised me that he would never hurt me and he's doing the opposite so it's only right that he endure some pain as well. With each step that led me closer to him, my mind began to change about stabbing him. This nigga wasn't worth me sitting in jail for the rest of my life, but hell hath no fury like a woman scorned. This was the second time I gave him a pass.

As I walked up the stairs, one by one, my mind changed again. I decided I was going to stab Hodari ass to death. My heart was bleeding from the pain he caused me, and I wanted to see his heart bleed literally. I wanted to see the look on his face once he discovered what a broken heart felt like. I didn't deserve to be treated like this and I was going to make sure he got the message, but once at the top of the stairs, I stopped and just threw the knife on the floor. I had other plans for him. I was going to give his ass something to remember every time the thought about sticking his dick into another woman. I tiptoed in the room and made my way over to the bed. I heard him snoring so that meant he was sound asleep. I pulled the cover from over his body, put crazy glue on his thigh, and stuck his dick to it. Hodari was going to learn to stop playing with my heart.

CHAPTER SEVENTEEN

"What the fuck is up with that," Apollo asked Nu-Nu. Apollo looked spaced out. He was looking like his soul was just taken away.

"I'm not sure what that's all about, but both of them need to be dealt with. Were my eyes deceiving me or did I see them two lock lips," Nu-Nu asked.

"Your eyes are not playing tricks on you, but ain't you fucking Hodari," Apollo quickly asked sounding puzzled.

Nu-Nu eyes drifted downward because before she responded. "Yea and I see that my sister don't give a fuck about me, you or her best friend. She's a dirty slut and I'm going to deal with her accordingly. I know exactly what to do to get her back."

"Me too," Apollo said as his hand drifted to Nu-Nu thigh.

She pushed his hand away quickly. "It's not that type of party homie."

Apollo laughed to lighten the moment. "I was just fucking with you," Apollo said lying through his teeth. If Nu-Nu had gone along with him, he would be all in her guts with no questions asked. "I don't know about you, but I'm about to go confront her," he said as he opened the door.

Nu-Nu reached over Apollo and closed his door. "Naw, you fall back. Let me handle things with Jaliyah and you go handle your boy."

"I got my boy don't worry about that, but Jaliyah is my bitch and I'm going to take care of that ass." Apollo said fuming.

"Are you serious right now Apollo. Did you fall and bump your head? Jaliyah is not your bitch or have you forgotten. Like I said I got her you just worry about your trifling ass so call friend." Nu-Nu looked at Apollo then said, "You know what, I think I will take you up on your offer. Let's play the same games they are playing. I know my sister still loves your dirty drawers so follow me."

Nu-Nu and Apollo got out the car and went to her apartment with one thing on their minds, revenge. Once upstairs, Apollo wanted so badly to go across the hall to Jaliyah's apartment. He wanted to make love to her for the last time, but after he saw Jaliyah and Hodari kiss, he knew it was officially over between them and he would never touch her again, not even with a ten-foot pole. There was no getting back together. She broke the code. He felt that it was cool for a nigga to fuck all the females in the world, but the minute a female mess with someone a man knows, it's the end of the fucking world. Niggas are so double standard.

"You have a nice place here," Apollo said as he walked around Nu-Nu crib. He admired everything he saw, from her great taste of furniture down to her decors. When his eyes landed on a picture that hung on her wall of three kids he asked, "Whose kids."

"Those are my kids. They live with their daddy. Ages 7, 5, and 2."

"I didn't know you had kids," Apollo replied.

"There are a lot of things people don't' know about me," Nu-Nu said as she grabbed his hand and led him to her bedroom.

Nu-Nu wasted no time getting undressed. Then she turned and helped Apollo get undress. He was moving just a little bit too slowly for her. She was ready to get their fuck session over with. She was feeling ashamed for what she was about to do, but it had to be done. She was about to try to fuck her pain away while in the process of hurting two people that she trusted the most.

Standing butt naked in her room, Nu-Nu walked over to her dresser and positioned her

IPhone while Apollo watched attentively. He was mentally taking notes in case he wanted to make a home video with him and Tina. She made sure she positioned it so it could capture all the right angles. She then walked over to her bed where Apollo laid with his rock hard dick and jumped on it. She rode his dick so good that he came in a matter of minutes. The footage on the camera was too short for her and plus, he wasn't going to be the only one walking away pleased. Nu-Nu jumped off Apollo's dick and she fell onto the bed. She told Apollo, "Your turn." He looked at her mysteriously. He had no clue as to what she was talking about until he saw her spread her legs apart. He wasted no time with burying his face in between her legs. With every lick and flick of the tongue, Nu-Nu screamed out his name just to add more effect to their homemade video. Once they finished their business. Apollo got dressed and headed out the door with no strings attached.

Once Apollo was gone, Nu-Nu felt like shit. Was it really worth her self-dignity to sleep with a man just to get back at her sister and the man she loved? She believed it was and there was no other way to get back at a person than to hurt them the same way they hurt you.

Nu-Nu knew her worth and wanted Hodari to see it. She saw a future with him, even though he didn't see one with her. She was trying to do everything in her power to get him to see she was the one, but Mariah had him blinded. She wanted so badly to make things work out with Hodari, but realization was starting to sink in that it would never happen. Nu-Nu began to feel depressed so she needed something to change her mood. She got out her bed, threw on her robe, and then headed to her living room to retrieve her purse. She then head back to her room with her purse thrown over her shoulder. Nu-Nu sat at the edge of her bed and unzipped her purse only to go to the side pocket to unzip that. Her eyes lit up once it landed on the alumni foil that carried her dope. Nu-Nu always kept a bag of dope handy. Nu-Nu wanted to get high to take the pain away. Instead of her shooting her dope into her veins like she normally did. She decided to put it up her nose.

After Nu-Nu got in her zone, she grabbed her phone off the dresser then jumped back in the bed. She watched the video and smiled because she knew she was about to cause some everlasting pain. Nu-Nu didn't waste any time editing the video than pressing the send button forwarding it to Apollo. Apollo responded with smiley face emoji's and that was her cue to forward the video to Jaliyah and Hodari. Nu-Nu wished she could be a fly on the wall when Hodari and Jaliyah received the video.

It was on to her next task. Mariah had finally accepted the phony friend request that Nu-Nu had sent her so she made a call to Mariah that she would never forget. At this point, Nu-Nu was in her glow so she laid back in her bed and drifting off to sleep.

****

After three hours, Nu-Nu woke up from her nap with evil thoughts on her mind. She decided to call her mom. She needed someone to talk to because she wasn't thinking rationally and she knew her mother would help make some sense of her situation.

"Momma, shit is crazy. I have more competition besides Mariah," Nu-Nu chatted into the phone.

"Girl, you know my time is money and if you want my advice on this lil love triangle, you already know what this is going to cost you," Darlene said while standing in her full length mirror taking her rollers out her hair.

"Why can't you just give me advice from the kindness of your heart like any other normal

163

mother? I'm your fucking daughter," Nu-Nu
screamed. "This is the least you can do. I don't
have to keep feeding your habit. I take care of my
own habit and you should be able to do the same,"
Nu-Nu spoke feeling like the world was on her
shoulder.

Her mother sighed then smacked her lips.
"Just this one time because you sound like you are
about to kill yourself over there," Darlene spoke as
if she was doing her daughter a huge favor.

Nu-Nu loves her mother with everything she
had in her, but she never understood why her
mother could never be like every other mother that
showed love, affection, and concern. She was a
part-time mother, with a habit who only cared
about one thing and it wasn't the well-being of her
child. Sometimes Nu-Nu wished it was her mother
that her aunt killed instead of her daddy because
she knew her aunt would have done a better job of
raising her and Jaliyah. The things that Nu-Nu was
allowed to get away with as a child should have
never been accepted. Nu-Nu never really felt that
motherly love from her mother. She felt a
friendship to a degree, but a motherly love no. This
is why Nu-Nu didn't know how to be a mother to
her own kids.

"I can't stand Jaliyah. She picked up your habit and when I catch her I'm putting my hands on her. I'm going to kill her," Nu-Nu said to her mom.

"What you mean she picked up my habit? Is she on drugs? If so, you're the one who probably turned her out because she's not around me often." Darlene said then smacked her lips.

"No she isn't on drugs. She picked up your hoe tendencies. She doing the same thing to me that you did to your sister."

My mom laughed. "Oh that habit. Girl, that's your sister, mistakes happens. You can't kill her over a dick. Get over it. There are plenty of dicks out here. Have you tried talking to Jaliyah," Darlene asked. "And just an FYI little girl, Jaliyah didn't pick up hoe tendencies from me, she got them from her momma. Her mom fucked my boyfriend before I fucked hers. I vowed to get her back for sleeping with my man when the time was right. I waited until she was married and happily in love and struck. All you have to do is fuck her man to get even. You will feel so much better, trust me it works."

Jaliyah didn't respond to what her mother had said because she had already slept with someone her sister loves and it didn't make her feel any better. Despite Nu-Nu's own hoe tendencies, she had a heart, she had feelings, and all she wanted was a man to call her own.

Nu-Nu ended the call with her mom by telling her "Thanks for the advice."

Once off the phone, Nu-Nu instantly got a headache. Her head was pounding. She had a lot going on through her mind and the only thing that was going to take her mind away was to get high. She picked up her phone and called her dope man so he could deliver her some goods.

Nu-Nu was a functional, fly girl type of dope head. She stayed dressed to impress. By looking at her, you wouldn't have known that she got high a couple of times out of the week, but lately she was getting high more than normal because of Hodari.

CHAPTER EIGHTEEN

I couldn't get any sleep. Reality was really setting in for me. My man was a liar and a cheater. He wasn't any different than the next man and Jaliyah tried to warn me. I felt so bad for snapping on her that day at the restaurant. All she was trying to do was protect my heart. Next time I saw her, I planned on giving her a well deserved apology.

I sat on the side of the bed all morning with my feet propped up on my chase and cried out my eyes until my tear ducts were drained. I didn't think I had another tear left in me. I was all cried out. Cutting an onion couldn't even get tears to come down my face. My eyes rotated around my room and my eyes sadden as they hit each angle. I thought my bedroom, our bedroom was going to be the best place in the house for Hodari and I. I assumed my over sized bedroom, that housed my beautiful black and white bedroom set, with the pretty decors to match was going to be the place where we created life. A special life that I could call my own.

The tears that I thought I no longer had came rushing down my face. They wouldn't stop falling even after I tried to blink them away. I wanted a family with Hodari. I wanted him to be my husband. I wanted a good life with him. The more I thought about all the things we could have had together, the angrier I got. Without thinking twice, I went down stairs, grabbed a big pot from the cabinet next to the stove, filled it with water than headed back upstairs. It was time I wake this cheating bastard up.

I stood over him with the pot in my hand and poured the water all in his face trying to drowed him. Hodari jumped up swinging and one of his hooks caught me in the face causing me to stumble back a little, but I didn't let that stop me, this wasn't the first nigga that put his hands on me. I could take a punch or two, but just as quickly as I got my balance, I stole on his ass back in his face, catching him off guard.

"Calm down, Mariah, what the fuck is going on," Hodari said as he threw his hands up in the air.

"You know what it is. You a liar and a cheater and this time I'm dead serious, it's over between us. I'm tired of your bitches contacting me." I sobbed.

"Baby, I told you Keisha is a shit starter. I'm going to handle her the next time I see her. She don't mean shit to me and I already told you that. It's her kids that I care about. I apologize. I apologize for keeping this huge secret because I see that it's hurting our relationship. I should have never fucked her when I took her the money for the kids. It's all my fault. It will never happen again. I love you Mariah, I swear I do." Hodari tried to walk toward me to embrace me, but I jumped back. I didn't want his dirty hand on me.

"The shit I'm talking about has nothing to do with Keisha and thanks for admitting to something that I already knew. You are making it just that much easier to walk away from you, but seriously this has nothing to do with Keisha. Another bitch you've been dicking down reached out to me earlier this morning."

"Wh..."Hodari tried to cut me off, but I over talked him.

"No matter how much I wanted to believe that you were different than any other man that I have come across, you found a way to prove me wrong. You have me questioning my on capablity when it comes to selecting men. Am I a magnet for hoe ass niggas. I wish I could blink your ass away, but I really want to meet these hoes personally to thank them for saving my life," I said as I continued to cry. "You hurt me. You hurt me real bad and the only reason why it hurt so bad is because I believed in you." Hodari tried to reach out to me again to comfort me and again, I took a jumped back. "Pack your clothes and get the hell out ."

"I'm not leaving until you tell me what's going on because I haven't been cheating on you," Hodari said calmly while lying through his teeth.

"You're a fucking liar and it's written all over your face."

I walked over to my dress and grabbed my phone to show Hodari the picture. The expression on his face answered all the questions that I had. "This is not what you think. This picuture is old."

"Nigga, I'm not trying to hear that. There is no reason to keep lying, just pack your shit and leave. I'm giving you 30 minutes to get your shit together and if you not gone by then, I'm calling 9-1-1 to come help you pack," I spoke with confidence. My tears had finally dried up. He wasn't worth another tear or was any other man. I refuse to let another man hurt me.

Hodari hit the wall and punched a hole in it and disappeared into the bathroom. Moments later I heard him scream, "What did you do to my dick." I didn't say a word. I was wondering when he was going to notice his dick was stuck to his leg. I guess he won't be using that for a while. Hodari stormed out the bathroom, grabbed his clothes he had on the day before, threw them on and headed out the door without packing his shit.

A sense of calmness came over me once he was out my presence These last weeks has been very trying for me. From Hodari constantly missing our appointments with the fertility clinic, finding out about Keisha and her kids, the chick with no identity and let me not forget about Traye. I wish I could click my heels together and be far away from everybody.

I was getting ready to start packing Hodari things for him, but I heard my phone ring. It was Jaliyah. I took a seat on my bed before I answered her call, then I quickly got back up. I took the sheets off the bed and tossed them across the room. I had planes to burn those sheets later.

"Hey boo, what's up," she asked.

At first I was going to lie and tell her nothing much because I didn't feel like talking about me and Hodari's situation at that very moment, but she was my best friend. I might as well kept it one hundred with her. "Everything, but the right thing is what's up. Life isn't perfect. It isn't all peaches and cream like I thought it would be," I spoke into the phone.

"What's wrong, "You know you can talk to me, " Jaliyah probed.

"It's Hodari again," I said ashamed.

"Is he alright," Jaliyah asked.

"Yes, he's okay. I'm the one that's not fine. You really tried to warn me about him and I'm sorry for not listening. He cheating and always has been."

"Is it with that Keisha chick." Jaliyah question.

"No," I answered quicky.

I heard Jaliyah take a deep breath. "Well do you know who it is?"

"No…I mean yes,…not really," I said not giving her a for sure answer. I went into details about the phone conversation and the picture that I received. I noticed the tone in her voice changed quickly. "Are you alright Jaliyah?"

"Yes, I'm fine. Why you ask that."

"If I didn't know any better it seem like you were relieved when I didn't say your name." I began to laugh and she joined in. I quickly changed the subject because I was tired of talking about that non-motherfucking factor Hodari. "I need you to meet me at the airport in an hour so I can take my rental car back. Once you picked me up from there, I need you to take me to the

172

autobody shop to pick up my car, then we can head back to my crib for some much needed drinks."

Jaliyah didn't have a problem with doing what I asked of her. She replied, "I can't wait until we make it back to your crib because I feel like drinking my life away." I laughed at her then hung up the phone.

That laugh felt so good, despite what I was going through. It seemed like I haven't had anything to laugh or even smile about in a while. All I know is, I miss having a smile on my face. I miss enjoying life and I really missed my best friend Jaliyah. For some apparent reason, Jaliyah have been very distance with me lately. Everytime I tried to reach out to her to spend some time, she was always busy. I wondered what was up with that. In the beginning, yes, I blamed it on her wedding incident, but it's months later and things still haven't gotten back on track with us. Maybe she was in love, hell, I don't know. Last time we really had a good conversation, she told me about some guy she's been dating so maybe he's the one that's getting all her time. Whatever it is, I was going to get my answers when she came over because our friendship isn't what it used to be.

****

Walking through the gates and onto the streets, I saw Jaliyah's car. She was patiently waiting for me. I jumped in the car and we embraced each other with a hug.

"Look in the back seat," she said.

When I turned my head and looked in the back seat, I noticed a black bag. That black bag could only mean one thing, liquor. I grabbed the fifth of Ciroc and the two cups out of the bags, opened the bottle and poured us each a drink. She pulled off from the curb and headed to the auto body shop.

Driving down Cicero Avenue this time of day was a headache. It was rush hour so it was going to take us longer than usual to get to where we needed to be. It didn't bother us though, we had the AC blowing, trap music playing and a drink in our hand. As Jaliyah pulled up to the red light on Jackson and Cicero, she spotted Apollo's car along with Tina on the passenger side going through the light heading East bound on Jackson. She looked at me and all I did was give her a nod of approval. Jaliyah immediately threw on her turn signal and proceed with cautions.

"So what's the plan," I asked.

"There is no plan…just give me a minute to think," Jaliyah said as she continued to follow the two people that she hated most in this world.

I picked up her cup from out of the cup holder and added a little bit more liquor in it and handed it to her. I was hoping that it would help speed up her thinking process, then I added more liquor to my cup as well. As we came up on Pulaski and Jackson, Jaliyah got caught at the light. She hit the steering wheel pissed because she thought we were going to loose them. We both tried our best to keep our eye on his car. We noticed that Apollo had pulled his car over at the next corner. Then we saw Apollo get out the car and walked over to Tina's side of the car and opened the door for her.

"This bitch ass nigga never opened the car door for me," Jaliya yelled out.

At that moment, I knew that Jaliyah was still in love with Apollo, but it was going to hurt to much for them to work things out between them. He caused her to much pain and the pain that he caused she will never forget. This is the exact way I was feeling about Hodari. I will always love Hodari, but I must walk away to keep my sanity.

The light had turned green and by this time Apollo and Tina were crossing the street. Jaliyah had put her feet on the gas pedal and pushed it all the way to the floor without thinking twice. In a matter of seconds, I heard a boom, then I saw Apollo and Tina's body fly into the air. I looked behind me and saw each one of their bodies hit the pavement. Jaliyah stopped the car instantly and our bodies jerked. She then put her car in reverse and drove over their bodies. I looked at Jaliyah with my mouth wide opened because I was shocked behind her actions. I thought she was finished, but it was more that needed to be done. The look on Jaliyah's face was disturbing, too disturbing that I was scared to say anything to her. She got out the car and I jumped out behind her without even thinking about the kind of trouble we were in. She walked over to there bodies and spit on each one of them and mouth the words, "Payback's a bitch."

"I walked off and got back in the car because a crowd was forming around. I yelled out to get Jaliyah's attention."Get your ass in the car before the police get here."

Jaliyah ran swiftly and got in the car. Something told me she wasn't finish yet. There was no icing on her cake. She had to add the finishing touch. She put her car in

drive and drove over their bodies once more. At this moment, I knew me nor Jaliyah was in our right state of mind because for one, I didn't try to stop Jaliyah from committing this crime of passion. The alcohol had taken over our thought process. If I was in my right state of mind, when we saw Apollo I would have told her to leave it alone and go straight to the autobody shop, but I didn't. All I did was add fuel to the fire by asking her "What's the plan."

The liquor gave Jaliyah a badge of bravery that I never seen before. "I told them I was going to get them especially that bitch Tina, but I owed Apollo double time. Now they can have my until death do us part."

Still shocked, I was now an accessory to two murders. All I could do was lean my seat back as far as it could go and think on how I was going to get myself out of this. I looked over at Jaliyah and I could tell she was in thinking mode as well. She just drove the car without saying a word. We headed to the autobody shop like nothing ever happened and went straight to my house to finish our drink.

CHAPTER NINETEEN

There was so much hatred building up inside of Hodari for Keisha and Nu-Nu that he wanted to kill them both with his bare hands. Once he figured out how to get the crazy glue off his dick, he was going to pay each one of them a visit.

Hodari pulled up at his crib that only Jaliyah knew about and rushed upstair and got on his laptop. He went straight to google trying to find a remedy to unstick his dick from his leg because he was just to embarrassed to go to the hospital. Once he found a quick remedy, he ran to the store and got what he needed. He rushed back home and applied the fingernail polish remover with acetone to the area and it removed instantly.

Hodari jumped in the shower and all he could do was think about Mariah. He was so made at himself for hurting the only woman that have truly loved him. He knew he couldn't let Mariah get away from him that easily so he had to put in some work to win her heart back. No matter what anybody thought, Hodari really did love Mariah.

As soon as Hodari got out of the shower, he heard his phone vibrating. He looked at it and noticed that it was Jaliyah calling him. He didn't feel like being bothered with Jaliyah so he ignored his phone and placed it back on his dresser. He sat on his bed so he could lotion up when he noticed his phone vibrating again. He looked at it again and again it was Jaliyah. He did the very same thing he did before, he ignored the call. Before he got a chance to sit the phone down, there it was vibrating again.

"Jaliyah, what is it. I got too much shit going on over here," Hodari barked into the phone.

"Trust me I know. I know all about your cheating ass, but what are we going to do about Nu-Nu and Apollo with this video."

"What video," Hodari asked puzzled.

"The video she sent to your phone," Jaliyah said. Nu-Nu had sent them a group text message this is how Jaliayah knew that he should have received the video as well.

Hodari had so much going on that he didn't even noticed that Nu-Nu had send a video to his phone. Hodari told Jaliyah to hold on while he go through his messages. He found the message that was from Nu-Nu. He put Jaliyah on speaker phone while he watched the video. Hodari smirked a little while watching the video. At the end of the video, Jaliyah made it known that coincidently her and

Apollo pulled up at the same time and saw them two kissing in the car.

Hodari was at a loss of words, but he didn't give to flying fucks about Nu-Nu fucking his boy because she wasn't his woman, they actually shared pussy quite often. Hodari was moreso worried about his boy's feelings because he was caught red handed kissing his guy ex-fiancee.

"Have you spoken to Apollo since this video?" Hodari asked Jaliyah.

"Nope," Jaliyah answered nervously and she wasn't going to volunteer him any additional information either. Jaliyah had never killed before so he tried to play it smooth as she talked to Hodari even though she have been a nervous wreck. She has been a nervous wreck since she ran Tina and Apollo down like a dog. She wasn't going to admit that to him or anybody else what she done. The only people that would know what happened are the people that was present.

Hodari asked his next question. "Have you spoken with Nu-Nu?"

Jaliyah replied with the same answer from her previous question, "Nope, but my question to you is what are we goin to do about Nu-Nu and Apollo for betraying us?"

"To be honest, absolutely nothing. They didn't betray me, they betrayed you. I know me and my guy will have some words about you because of the type of relationship y'all had, but that shit with Nu-Nu will be a joke for us. Fact of the matter is, Nu-Nu isn't my woman and she can swing that pussy anyway she like. Now, what I'm going to do is beat the shit out of Nu-Nu for contacting my girl," Hodari said with some assurance in his voice.

Jaliyah wasn't to impress with Hodari's response, but she was happy that Hodari was going to beat Nu-Nu ass even if it didn't have anything to do with the video. Jaliyah and Hodari ended their call and went on with their day as usual.

****

Hodari grabbed his keys from his pocket and searched for the one that would let him into Nu-Nu's apartment. He found the key and put it into the lock, but for some apparent reason, it didn't work. He looked at the key strangely. He knew he had the right key because he had used it on numerous occasions. Just to satisfy his curiosity, Hodari tried the key one more time and again, it didn't work. Then it hit him that Nu-Nu had changed her locks. He was pissed. He so badly wanted to be waiting for her in her crib when she arrived. He wanted to catch her off guard and beat the shit out of her.

Nu-Nu was no dummy, she knew she fucked up big time so she was going to do everything in her power to avoid him until she got Mariah out the way then he had no choice, but to run into her arms. Hodari stood in Nu-Nu hallway and called her phone to see if she would pick up and she didn't. At this point, there wasn't anything Hodari could do so he left Nu-Nu's apartment, jumped in his car and headed over to Keisha's house.

As Hodari drove through traffic, the only person that invaded the space in his mind was Mariah. He was really upset with himself for hurting the woman he love. He knew that he had some making up to do so he called his personal jeweler and told him that he needed a ring made for Mariah. He trusted his jeweler's judgement so he left the designing of the ring in his hands.

Pulling up in front of Keisha's south side apartment, Hodari frowned as he saw the local drug dealers standing in front of her building. Keisha lived in a drug infested neighborhood and for some apparent reason it seemed like she didn't want to get away. Hodari had given Keisha money to move because he didn't want his kids growing up in that neighborhood. According to Keisha, she never moved because her credit wasn't good so recently he gave her some money to clean her credit now he's waiting to see what her excuse is going to be this time.

Hodari got out the car and headed into Keisha's two flat building and repeated, the same routine he did when he was at Nu-Nu's crib. He grabbed his keys out his pocket and search for the key that would let him in. He turned the key and the door opened without any hesitation unlike Nu-Nu's door.

"Is that you Hodari," Keisha called out.

Hodari didn't say a word. He searched each room looking for his kids. He was so protective over the kids that he didn't want them to witness him beating the shit out of their mother. From the looks of it, the kids were gone.

"Where the kids?" Hodari asked.

Keisha walked out the kitchen smiling, "They're at my moms house."

"Good," he said then smack the shit out of her causing her to fall in to the wall.

"Hodari stop," Keisha yelled, as she witnessed him getting closer to her, but he didn't listen. He kept putting his paws on her.

Keisha fell to the floor and bald up in a fetus position to try to protect her face from the blows he was throwing her way.

"Why are you doing this to me? What did I do?" she screamed out.

Hodari didn't answer any questions or giving an explanation on why he was beating her ass. There really was no need to. Keisha knew the answer to her own questions. She knew how he felt about Mariah and she knew the moment she reached out to her there would be repercussions that followed. What she didn't know was that he was going to come and beat her the way he did. Hodari beat her like a man and stomped her like dirt. He stomped her until she began to see stars. Keisha grabbed his shirt trying to stop him, but it only caused him to get angrier when he heard his shirt rip so she began choke her. She reached up and scratched Hodari in his face and he instantly let her go. Keisha felt like she was at an advantage at this point so she built up enough courage and swung on Hodari causing him to taste his own blood. Hodari's reflex kicked in and he stole Keisha in her mouth chipping her front tooth. Keisha tried to crawl her way into the kitchen to get a knife, but Hodari wasn't going to let that happen. He stomped her a couple more times before he heard a neighbor at the door. He stopped instantly when he heard one of Keisha's neighbor yell out through the thin walls, "The police is one their way."

Hodari looked at Keisha. "When the police get here, you better not give them my name. If you do, you can raise them bastard ass kids of yours by your damn self."

After that Hodari didn't say another word. He left out the door in search for Nu-Nu.

CHAPTER TWENTY

Time was exactly 11:45 p.m. when Nu-Nu pulled up on the dark quiet suburban street. The only lights that could be seen were a couple of porch lights and lights from a couple of televisions, but Nu-Nu didn't let that stop her from what she was about to do. The only lights she was concerned with was the house she was about to burn to the ground and she was hoping Mariah was in. Nu-Nu didn't see Mariah's car in sight so she guessed it was parked in the garage, but when Nu-Nu got closer to the porch, she froze in her steps. She noticed a for rent sign stuck in the window.

"Shit," she cursed out loud as she stood in front of the house.

"Can I help you," she heard a man's voice say. Nu-Nu turned around and was face-to-face with the older white man from the other day who was on on the porch with his wife when she vandalized Mariah's car.

Nu-Nu was caught totally off guard. She had to think quickly because she had a gasoline container in her hand. "Umm, I was just looking for my friend that used to live here and I didn't realized she moved. I haven't spoken to her in a while. I was in the neighborhood when I ran out of gas and I just knew she was going to be here to help me," Nu-Nu said lying without thinking twice."

"If you want, I can take you to get some gas," the man said politely.

"I don't want to cause you any trouble. I have another friend that don't live to far away and he can come help me, but thanks for the offer," Nu-Nu replied.

"Wait right here," I'll be right back.

Nu-Nu stood there looking strangely. She didn't know if she should wait or leave, but when she finally made the decision to leave, the man was back with a torn off sheet of paper in his hand.

"Here," he said as he handed Nu-Nu the paper.

"What this," she asked curiosity.

"That's your friend's new address. I have my own lawn service and I serviced her lawn the other day. I'm sure she will be glad to hear from you," the man said.

Nu-Nu felt like she had just hit the mega-millions three times. "Thank you so much she shouted.

Nu-Nu walked to her car and got in. She watched the man out of her rear view mirror as he walked back to his house, onto his porch and then into his house. Nu-Nu didn't waste anytime starting her car up and pulling off in in the direction to Nu-Nu house.

Riding down Roosevelt and jumping onto 1-355, Nu-Nu headed to the northwest suburbs to destroy Mariah and Hodari. She knew that if she killed or brought any harm to Mariah, Hodari's world would come tumbling down and that was her plan. She wanted Hodari to suffer. She wanted him to witness love and have it taken away from him, knowing there wasn't anything that he could do about it.

Nu-Nu tried to convince herself over and over that after finding out Hodari was sleeping with her sister, she no longer wanted to be with him, but the truth of he matter was, Nu-Nu craved Hodari. She breathe Hodari and she definitely couldn't see herself without Hodari. No matter what he did to her or who he sleeps with, she couldn't see herself without him, but there was one problem. The video she sent. Nu-Nu was starting to regret taking Apollo up on his offer. Whatever possible future her and Hodari could have had together, she could toss that out the window.

Getting off at exit 4, Biesterfield Road, Nu-Nu felt a lump form in her throat. She was nervous about what she was about to do, but it had to be done. She followed her GPS direction until she was in front of a georgous brick house. The house was huge and Nu-Nu instantly became jealous. Mariah had everything Nu-Nu wanted and more. The luxury car, the house, the man and from what she could see, pure happiness. Nu-Nu thought that Mariah had it made, but what she didn't know, Mariah worked hard for everything she had. She turnt her trials into tribulations and her tests into testimonies. Yes, Hodari was a good provider, but with or without him, she could hold her own.

Nu-Nu parked her car a couple of houses form Mariah house scoping out the neighborhood. Unlike Mariah's old neighborhood, it was pitch black in Schaumburg. There wasn't a light insight. Not a street light, no porch light, not nothing. After she finished scoping out the neighborhood, she focused on Mariah's house. She noticed only Mariah's car in her driveway and that was a good thing. There was no Hodari there to try to save her. Nu-Nu was so ready to get this over with now that she had built up enough nerves. Nu-Nu could here her mother's voice loud and clear telling her to kill Nu-Nu. Even though Nu-Nu never listened to her mother before and she knew it was the wrong thing to do, Nu-Nu felt like this was the best advice that her mother could have ever given her. Nu-Nu was ready to send Mariah's house up into flames.

Nu-Nu reached on the passenger side, onto the floor, and grabbed her gasoline container. She then placed it on the passenger seat. She closed her eyes, took a deep breathe and asked the man upstairs for her forgiveness for the crime she was about to commit. Then all of a sudden, a sense of nervousness came over her, Nu-Nu's hands began to shake and her throat became dry. Nu-Nu was about to chicken out. She didn't know if she could go through with her plan. Her mind was racing a mile a minute. Nu-Nu felt all she needed was some water to calm her nerves so she started up her car and headed to the closest gas station her GPS found. She ended up at a Shell gas station that was only about five minutes away.

"Do you have a bathroom I can use," Nu-Nu asked the Indian man that was behind the counter.

"Yes," he said then pointed to the back of the store.

Nu-Nu grabbed a bottle of FIJI water out of the refrigerator as she headed to the bathroom and yelled out, "I'll pay for this on my way out." Then she closed the bathroom door behind her.

Once in the bathroom, Nu-Nu stared at herself in the mirror. She didn't recognize the person staring back at her. *How did it get to this point*, Nu-Nu questioned the image that was staring back at her. She almost was about to say fuck it and walk away, but then she thought about Hodrari. She thought about all the times he hurt her and she thought about all the times he showed her love. Nu-Nu stood their shaking her head. She was confused. She started to question the love Hodari had for her, but one thing she was certain of, was the love she had for him and now it was time she do the unthinkable all in the name of love.

Nu-Nu finally took a sip of her water to satisfy her thirst. Next, she took a couple of deep breathes to try to calm her nervousness that had come over her, but it didn't work. She began to sweat profusely. She used the back of her hand and wiped the sweat away, but more sweat followed. Nu-Nu threw her head back and look up at the ceiling and brushed her hands over her face. Nu-Nu knew what she had to do to get rid of her nervousness. She took a couple steps over to the toilet and let the lid down and took a seat. She opened her purse and pulled out the one thing that has never let her down or never failed her.

Exiting the bathroom, Nu-Nu felt more confident than ever, she got in line to pay for her water and exit the gas station. As she was walking to her car, her and Hodari eyes locked while he stood at the pump, pumping his gas.

CHAPTER TWENTY-ONE

"Mariah, if the police come looking for us, we don't know shit and ain't seen shit. We have been at your house all day. We in this together. We are each other alibi," she spoke. I guess I didn't reply fast enough so she asked, "Do you hear me?"

"Yea, I hear you loud and clear Jaliyah because I'm not trying to sit behind bars for two murders I didn't commit. I can't believe you killed them. This shit is crazy. Love will have people do some crazy things." I paused for a minute and studied Jaliya's gesture before I proceeded. "I really had no idea you was going to take it this far. Beat him and the bitch ass yea, cut some tires, bust out some windows, but killing them, that shit was over the top. Regardless of what you did, you my girl and I got your back."

"Bitch, what the fuck that supposed to mean. Fuck you and fuck love. Love didn't make me kill them, they made me kill them for the shit they did to me," Jaliyah said as the word slurred off her tongue. "If I go down, trust and believe you going down with me. Like I said we are in this together," she giggled a little.

I was shocked behind her remarks, but I took it as if the liquor was talking. "I'm not trying to argue with you so chill out. Jaliyah, you're drunk. Just lay down for a minute," I pleaded with her.

Jaliyah grabbed the fifth of Ciroc off the table and turnt it upside down as the poison trickled down her throat to the very last drop. "Lay down my ass. I'm out this bitch," Jaliyah said then stormed out my door.

I'm not going to lie, I didn't even try to stop her. I was so happy when Jaliyah finally left. All I could do was pray she made it home safely.

After she left, I sat on my couch and thought long and hard on what my next move was going to be. As much as I hated to do it, I knew I had to call Hodari. For some reason, I felt I owed him this. I felt in my heart that I should be the first person to tell him about what happened to his friend despite our circumstances. Apollo and Hodari were like brothers so I knew he was going to take it hard, this is why it had to come from me. He might even hate me for being there, but I had to let him know what happened. My soul told me our relationship was over so at this point, I didn't care what he thought of me. If he did hate me, that was my ticket out.

I couldn't get my mind off Tina and Apollo. I really started to feel guilty for not stopping Jaliyah from running them down like dogs, but hell, what could I have done to stop her. Nothing at all, I convinced myself to believe so I picked up my phone and called Hodari and on the first ring he answered.

"Baby, I'm sorry," he sincerely said into the phone.

"Hodari, I'm not trying to hear that shit, but I need to talk to you about something very important. Can you come by?"

"Yes, baby first chance I get I'm there. Let me finishing handling this business and then I'm on my way to you."

"Ok," I replied then hung up the phone.

I didn't want to give Hodari a long winded conversation because I didn't want him to think we were back cool. We were far from being back on good terms.

CHAPTER TWENTY-TWO

After killing Tina and Apollo, Jaliyah was too exhausted to go after Nu-Nu. She was going to leave Nu-Nu to Hodari. Jaliyah knew that once Hodari got his hands on Nu-Nu, the ass beating she receive would be one she would never forget. All Jaliyah cared about at that point was getting as far away from Chicago as possible. She couldn't stand to be in Chicago another day. Jaliyah felt if she stayed in Chicago, the police would be looking for her soon and she wasn't about to go down for anybody's murder. Jaliyah rushed and packed all of her things, even though sure wasn't sure of where she was headed. She ran from room to room grabbing all her important things that she thought she would need and soon after she tried her best to disappear from the face of the earth.

****

"You dirty bitch," Hodari said as he charged at Nu-Nu.

Even though seeing Hodari wasn't expected, she didn't even try to run. She simply went in her purse and pulled out her blade. "Nigga if you touch me, I'm going to cut you."

Nu-Nu words stopped Hodari dead in his tracks. He had to think rationally. He wanted to beat the shit out of her, but at the same time he didn't want to get cut.

"You know I'm going to beat your ass so you better make sure you have that blade with you at all time," Hodari yelled out in frustration. He never thought he would have ran into Nu-Nu in the burbs. He had been searching high and low for her all day just to give her the ass beating she deserved.

"Hodari ain't nobody scared of you and I promise you if you walk up on me, now or any other time, I'm going to carve my name in your face to let all the hoes know you my property bitch." Nu-Nu was talking super tough and it had a lot to do with the dope in her system.

"So now you tough huh, I'm not about to sit here and argue with you. Just know I'm beating that ass sooner than later," Hodari said as he turn around to finish pumping his gas.

Nu-Nu thought about what Jaliyah told her about Hodari starting a family with Mariah and that pushed her over the edge. It really tortured her soul that he pushed her down the stairs and caused her to loose her baby. She ran up behind Hodari and Hodari heard her coming. He quickly turned around as soon as Nu-Nu swung the blade slicing him in the face. Hodari felt the wetness dripping down his face and instantly went into attack mode. He wrapped his hands firmly around her neck, cutting off her oxygen while quickly snatching the knife out of her hand tossing it to the ground. Nu-Nu couldn't breathe and he saw it in her eyes, but he didn't care. He wanted the bitch to suffer not die so he quickly let her go then smack her to the ground.

Nu-Nu's eyes landed on the knife, she grabbed it and sliced him across his right leg, but she didn't stop there. She sliced him a couple more times and blood gushed out everywhere. Hodari wanted to scream out in pain, but he didn't. He fought through the pain and snatched the knife out of her hand, but not before getting his fingers sliced. While still on the ground Hodari kick her in her abdomen and she dumped over in pain. He kicked her several more time and then he started to throw some punches.

"Leave that woman alone," Hodari heard a male's voice say.

He looked to the right of him and noticed the gas station worker had come out trying to play captain save a hoe with a bat in his hand. Hodari looked at the man like he was stupid, but then realized he was in the burbs and he didn't want any trouble so he got off Nu-Nu, headed to his car, and pulled off quickly.

Nu-Nu rushed from the ground and jumped into her car and followed Hodari. She looked at herself in the mirror and noticed the damaged he done to her face. She had a swollen lip, face and black eye. Under no circumstance was Nu-N going to allow him to get away with that. As she looked ahead she noticed that Hodari was caught by a red light. She smashed the pedal as far as it could go so she could catch him before the light turned green.

Pulling up on the side of his car, Nu-Nu quickly threw her car in park and jumped out the car with the gasoline can in her hand. She didn't waste anytime with pouring the gasoline on his car. Before Hodari realized what she was going. She lit fire to his car.

CHAPTER TWENTY-THREE

Four Months Later

"How you feeling baby," I said to Hodari as I nursed him back to health. I had just changed his bandages for his legs and back.

"I'm feeling great, thanks to you my love," Hodari said to me and he tapped me on my ass.

"Well, you know the routine, I'm off to work and if you need anything just give me a call.

"Okay, my love...I love you."

"Love you too," I said meaning every word of it.

It had been a trying four months for me since Hodari's accident, but by the grace of God my man is still here. Things could have been far more worst than what they are. This is his second time being burnt in a car. I'm just happy the police found Nu-Nu before I did and placed that bitch in jail for an attempt murder and arson. She will not be seeing the light of day anytime soon. Even though I'm happy that Nu-Nu is in jail and Hodari and I are back in a happy place, it took a lot out of me, to over look the things he had done. I have found it in my heart to forgive him, but I don't think I will ever forget.

Hodari had finally man up and told me about all his cheating ways. I told him he had to tell me everything by answering all my questions if he wanted us to move forward and he did just that while promising me that he will never hurt me again. He even told me that he didn't want to have anything else to do with Keisha's kids and I smiled and cried tears of joy. At that very instance, I knew where his loyalty lies, but I knew how much the kids meant to him and I told him I wanted to love her kids just as much as he loved them. Them kids needed him, they needed us and it would have been very selfish of me to take him out of the kids life. From that point on, I believed every single word that came out of his mouth. Hodari had me right back where he wanted me, especially after he got down on bended knee through his pain.

There were no complaints, life was good. It was definitely back on track, but one person was missing out of it and that was Jaliyah. I have reached out to her on several occasion and she have not answered or even made an attempt to return my calls. I missed my best friend dearly and all I could do was hope she was somewhere safe.

Jumping into my car, I turned the heat on blast. It was the beginning of winter. I hated winter. I've been tryin to get Hodari to move to a warmer climate, but he wasn't having it. He was going to be a Chicago nigga until the day he died. We had received a winter advisory the day before to be aware of the ten inches of snow that was coming and the dropping temperature later on that night. Under normal circumstance, I would have stayed home from work, but there were some important depositions that I had to get together and file at the clerks office. The snow was starting to come already and I couldn't wait until this work day was over.

I got in the office and did my work quicker than what I expected. I was so happy that I could leave work early. I thought about calling Hodari to let him know I was leaving early, but I wanted to surprise him. I made a quick stop at Victoria Secrets and got me a nice lingerie set in his favorite color, red. Then I stopped and picked up some groceries so I could cook his favorite meal, mozzarella stuffed chicken parmesan. It was going to be all about Hodari once I got home. I couldn't belive this man made me fall in love with him all over again.

As I pulled my car on the side of Hodari's in the drive way, all I thought about was chilling with my man and reassuring him that my love for him was real. I wanted to let him know that our bond will never be broken again.

Walking into the house, I set my bags on the kitchen counter, then called out Hodari's name, but there was no answer. My house was just to damn big for the two of us so I decided to call his phone to let him know I was home. When I didn't get an answer, I assumed he was sleep. I headed upstair to our room just to peak in on him. The closer I got to the room I began to hear voices. For a second, I thought it was the television, but when I recognized the voice that was coming from my bedroom my heart stopped.

"Fuck this pussy Hodari. I've missed you so much," I heard Jaliyah say. What the fuck she mean, she miss him so much. Hodari was my man. She had no business missing him.

"Girl, you know I miss you and this pussy," I heard Hodari say. I couldn't believe my ears. It felt like a ton of breaks had fell on me again. I couldn't believe I trusted him again and he turned back around and hurt me more than ever. How could he do this to me? How could they do this to me?

I couldn't stand by to hear another word of their sexcapade. I took care of this nigga and nursed him back to health and this is how he repays me. I quickly stormed off and headed to the basement where Hodari kept all of his guns. I returned back upstairs in a matter of seconds. My tears blurred my vision and I went in shooting without saying a word. The first bullet hit Jaliyah in the arm then she screamed out in pain, but the next bullet hit the wall. I'm not going to lie I wish that bullet had hit her in the head. I was really hurt for what they were doing to me. I know I got them off guard. They thought they could just be bold and disrespectful and fuck in my house without getting caught. The nerve of them two.

"Wait Mariah this isn't what you think," Hodari said as he put his hands up in the air, jumped off the bed, and began to walk toward me. "Put the gun down baby."

"If you know what's best for you, you will stop walking toward me." Hodari froze in his step instantly because the gun was now pointed at him. Then I began to giggle through the pain, "Nigga that's your favorite line. It is what I think. I'm not fucking blind. How can you do this to me?" I then turned my attention on Jaliyah. " I was your sister, your best friend, your rid or die. Remember, we was in this shit together." Then I turned my attention back to Hodari, " The hoe you fucking is the one that ran your friend and his bitch down," I screamed out.

Hodari just stood their with his mouth wide opened. He never got a chance to say his last goodbyes to Apollo because he was in the hospital. Hodari never really knew what happened beside Apollo and Tina got hit by a car and the police was still investigating the accident with no leads. There were plenty of times I wanted to tell Hodari what happened, but we was in a good place and I couldn't have him hating me.

My brain started to process all the stupid shit I've done and pointed it out when it came to Hodari. I was stupid for loving this nigga. I was stupid for giving him my heart, I was stupid for taking him back. I was stupid for being loyal to him. I was stupid for nursing him back to health. I was stupid for ever believing in him and the list went on. I was stupid on so many levels.

As my mind kept processing all the stupid things when it came to Hodari. I pointed the gun back in Hodari's direction and let three rounds off without thinking twice. After shooting him, the gun fell to the floor and Jaliyah took that opportunity to run for her life.

"Now momma, you have the truth and nothing, but the whole truth coming out of my mouth. See, I never really wanted to hurt anybody, but as you can see, I was hurting internally. Hodari pushed me to that point. All I wanted was for Hodari to love me and only me. I know this is a lot to grasp and there is no excuse for what I've done because I wasn't raised this way. You definitely taught me right from wrong so yes, I could have walked away, but the rage in me wouldn't allow me to."

My mom tears wouldn't stop flowing down her face. Her eyes were now puffy from all the crying she had been doing since I've been telling her the story of how I ended up in jail. I know she was hurting and so was I, but there was nothing that either one of us could do to ease the pain because the damage was done.

My mom took my face into her hand. "I understand," was the only words that escaped her mouth.

For the first time since telling her the story, I finally broke down because that's all I wanted was for her to understand why I did what I did. To this day, I still can't believe that all the time I was loving him, he was busy in the street loving on someone else.

Moral of the story

Men cheat, Women cheat, WE all cheat…
SO FUCK LOVE…No one is to be trusted.

CHECK OUT OTHER BOOKS BY SHONEY K

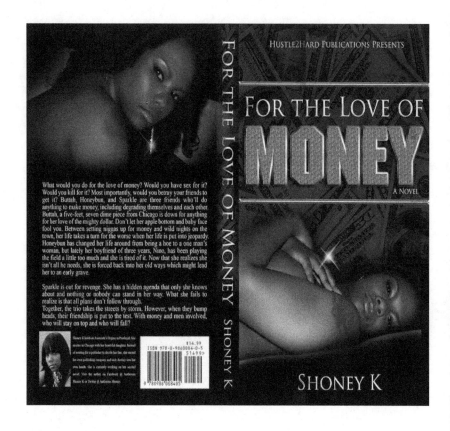

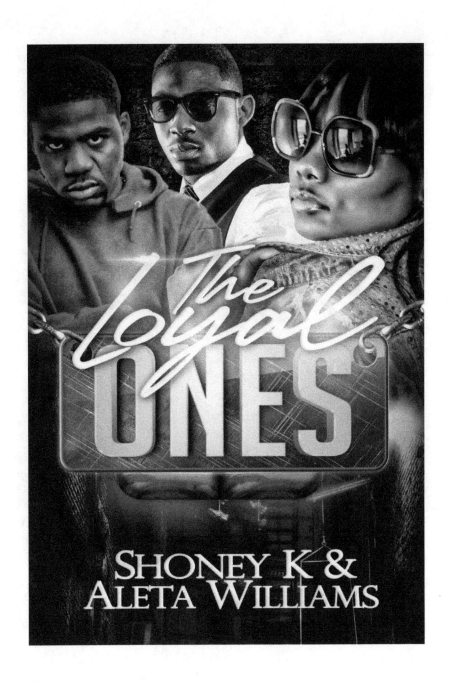

The Loyal ONES

SHONEY K &
ALETA WILLIAMS

HOW FAR WILL YOU *RIDE*
FOR YOUR NIGGA?

Riding Dirty

SHONEY K

CPSIA information can be obtained
at www.ICGtesting.com
Printed in the USA
LVHW080604130120
643361LV00015BA/1054/P